O

"When night covers the land,

"and we go our separate ways, I'll stand by my window and think of you." His lips touched her temple, her cheek, lighting a fire deep inside her. "And if you've any heart at all, you'll stir in your sleep and wish I was here beside you."

She moved her face, loving the feel of his lips on her skin. At her movement, he drew her closer and kissed the tip of her nose.

Her eyes widened, meeting his amber gaze. She was drowning in those golden depths. "Kiss me, Kirsten."

Dear Reader,

Spellbinder! That's what we're striving for. The editors at Silhouette are determined to capture your imagination and win your heart with every single book we publish. Each month, six Special Editions are chosen with *you* in mind.

Our authors are our inspiration. Writers such as Nora Roberts, Tracy Sinclair, Kathleen Eagle, Carole Halson and Linda Howard—to name but a few—are masters at creating endearing characters and heartrending love stories. Their characters are everyday people—just like you and me—whose lives have been touched by love, whose dreams and desires suddenly come true!

So find a cozy, quiet place to read, and create your own special moment with a Silhouette Special Edition.

Sincerely,

The Editors
SILHOUETTE BOOKS

RUTH LANGAN
Whims of Fate

Silhouette Special Edition

Published by Silhouette Books New York

America's Publisher of Contemporary Romance

To my daughter Mary Margaret
May you live happily ever after.

SILHOUETTE BOOKS
300 East 42nd St., New York, N.Y. 10017

Copyright © 1986 by Ruth Langan

ISBN: 0-373-09354-3

First Silhouette Books printing December 1986

America's Publisher of Contemporary Romance

Printed in the U.S.A.

RUTH LANGAN

enjoys writing about modern men and women who are not afraid to be both strong and tender. Her sense of humor is evident in her work. Happily married to her childhood sweetheart, she thrives on the chaos created by two careers and five children.

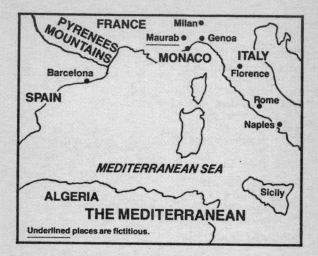

FRANCE
Milan •
PYRENEES
MOUNTAINS
Maurab • • Genoa
MONACO
ITALY
Barcelona •
Florence
SPAIN
Rome •
Naples •

MEDITERRANEAN SEA

ALGERIA
THE MEDITERRANEAN
Sicily
Underlined places are fictitious.

MICHIGAN
LAKE ERIE
Toledo •
• Cleveland
Akron •
FAIRCHILD
OHIO
Dayton •
• Columbus
Cincinnati •
Underlined places are fictitious.
KENTUCKY
WEST VIRGINIA

Chapter One

Once upon a time, in a land far away—"

"Why do all fairy tales start like that?" the four-year-old interrupted.

"Like what?" Kirsten paused in her reading and winked at the elderly woman across the room, who had looked up from her mending.

"'Once upon a time, in a land far away.' Why don't they say 'Today, in Ohio?'" The little girl formed the name of the state carefully, pursing her lips as she had been taught.

Laughing, Kirsten explained patiently, "Because these stories are pretend. They don't really happen. Especially today, in Ohio."

"I wish they would," the little girl murmured, snuggling against the shoulder of the young woman who held her on her lap. "Wouldn't it be fun to meet a handsome prince and become the queen of the land and live in a beautiful castle?''

"Umm." Kirsten smoothed the fine blond hair of the drowsy child and turned the page. She understood the little girl's imaginings; she'd had her own share of fantasies. But with discipline, she'd learned to temper dreams with a large dose of reality. "'... when the sun shone warm on all the fair people of the land...'"

As the rich voice droned on, the old woman watched her grandchild slowly nod off to sleep. Lifting her from Kirsten's arms, she murmured, "You're a dear to read to Amy after the full day you've put in."

"I don't mind, Mrs. Johnson."

Holding the little girl against her ample bosom, Mrs. Johnson sighed. "But all those questions. You must get enough of them from your second graders every day, without having to put up with more of Amy's after dinner."

Kirsten picked up a stack of papers. "I enjoy the questions. They show a quick mind. But now I'd better get back to my work. I promised the class I'd have their homework papers graded by tomorrow."

As the young woman climbed the stairs to her small upstairs apartment, the older woman sighed and muttered to her husband, "That one ought to be having babies of her own, instead of teaching other people's children. I've never seen such a natural with little ones."

"You're only her landlady, not her kin. Don't meddle, Rose. And don't rush things. A pretty little thing like Kirsten is bound to have plenty of men show an interest in her."

"Humpf." Rose settled her granddaughter among the quilts and watched as her husband dropped a kiss on the sleeping child's cheek.

They'd been caring for their grandchild since their daughter's accident. There would always be room in their home for a few extra strays.

"She's been teaching here in Fairfield for four years now. Must be twenty-five or twenty-six. By that age we'd been married for six years and had three children."

With twinkling eyes, he drew her close. "That's 'cause I couldn't stay away from the prettiest girl in Fairfield."

"Oh, you." Despite her protest, Rose hugged him before turning for a last glance at her sleeping granddaughter. Turning off the light, she followed her husband from the room. "Kirsten's been out of circulation too long. Spent her high school and college days rushing back to the farm to take care of her grandmother after that stroke. Now she spends all her time teaching and coaching sports on the weekends. Sports." Rose's tone showed her disapproval. "How's a talented woman like Kirsten ever going to find the right man if she spends every weekend coaching baseball and track in Fairfield, Ohio?"

"The right man will just have to find her. It's been that way from the beginning of time, Rose."

Upstairs, completely oblivious to their conversation, the object of their concern worked long into the night, completing class assignments. A drift of hair the color of ripe wheat fell nearly to her waist. Blue eyes, full of intelligence and humor, scanned each paper. Despite the lateness of the hour, she took the time to write little notes of encouragement in the margins before finally glancing up at the sound of the midnight chimes tolling from the old cathedral. Wearily she tumbled into bed.

"I've finished all the chalkboards, Miss Stevens. Now will you give me some batting practice?"

Kirsten looked up from her desk to study the somber face of the little boy in the doorway. Every day since the snow had begun melting, Danny Jenson had offered to stay after school and help with her classroom chores in exchange for baseball tips.

Kirsten had a special place in her heart for children like Danny. He was small for his age, and rail thin. His mother worked in a local diner and catered parties on weekends. His father, a trucker, had died in a highway accident two years ago. There was a thirteen-year-old sister, but she had her hands full taking care of the house and baby-sitting on weekends to earn spending money. Kirsten understood Danny's loneliness.

"Come on," Kirsten said, pushing her chair away from the desk. She'd just have to make time to finish her paperwork after the parent-teacher meeting. "I think it's time you learned how to drive one out of the ballpark."

With a grin, Danny picked up his mitt and followed his favorite teacher out to the frozen schoolyard.

It was nearly six o'clock when Kirsten walked the nine blocks to the Johnsons' boarding house. The light from the street lamps glistened in the patches of snow that clung stubbornly to the ground around bushes and evergreens. As she walked up the porch steps, the wonderful aroma of chicken stew and dumplings mingled with the scent of wood smoke in the frosty air.

Kirsten thought how fortunate she was to have found a haven in the Johnsons' cozy place. At first, when she'd been notified that her grandmother's farm would have to be sold for back taxes, Kirsten had faced a bleak future. Except for Gram, she had no family. All her savings had gone into paying Gram's medical expenses and maintaining the family holding. There were still times, late at night when her energy was sapped, that she gave in to her terrible grief at the loss of Gram and the farm. But she never allowed herself to dwell on the past. Now that she was in Fairfield, with a comfortable room and a job she enjoyed, her enthusiasm for life bubbled over.

"You're late." Rose lifted a whistling kettle from the stove.

"Parent-teacher meeting tonight. I wanted to put the best papers on each student's desk so the parents could see how hard they've been working."

"That kept you till dark?"

Kirsten grinned at Frank and ruffled Amy's hair. "Played a little ball with Danny Swenson first."

Frank looked interested. "How's he hitting them?"

"Better. He was afraid of the ball at first. Now he's developing a nice swing."

"You got some mail," Rose said, carrying a heaping platter to the table. "Registered letter. I had to sign for it." She carefully removed the oven mitts she was wearing, then looked up. "I put it on the hall table."

Surprised, Kirsten hurried to the hall and stared at the legal-sized envelope. Her mouth went dry. Trouble, she thought, remembering the official notice she'd received about the unexpected sale of the farm. This could only be bad news. Swallowing back her fear, she tore open the envelope and removed the letter.

Turning toward the light, she read:

Dear Ms. Stevens: Congratulations. Your entry in the Foodworld Supermarket Sweepstakes was randomly drawn, making you the grand prize winner of a two-week, all-expense-paid vacation in glamorous Maurab. To be valid, this prize must be claimed within two months. For further information, please phone, toll free, 1-800-555-1111.

Kirsten read the letter twice, then, more slowly, a third time. Mechanically she walked back to the dining room. Seeing her stunned expression, Rose cast a quick glance across the table at her husband.

"Something wrong?"

"I won a contest." Kirsten handed the letter to Rose, who read it quickly, then passed it to Frank.

"Foodworld," Rose said. "I remember those entry blanks when the new store opened. September, wasn't it?"

Kirsten nodded and began to spoon chicken stew onto her plate. "I stopped in for some school supplies. Tissues, paper towels. The clerk handed me an entry blank at the checkout counter."

"Me too." Rose smiled, revealing a dimple at each cheek. "Always enter those dumb things. Never expect to win anything."

"Looks official to me," Frank muttered, turning the letter over. "You going to call that number?"

"Course she's going to call," Rose insisted. "Nobody turns down a free trip."

Kirsten shrugged. "I'll call tomorrow. I'm sure there's a gimmick. I probably have to buy a hundred dollars' worth of dog food or something."

"Why don't you call now?" Rose urged.

Kirsten glanced at her watch. "It's probably too late."

She was putting it off, she realized. For a little while it would be fun to savor the dream before the phone call revealed the truth.

"The number's toll free. No harm done if nobody answers." Rose's dinner was forgotten now in her excitement.

Seeing her eager expression, Kirsten forced a smile. "All right. But just to satisfy your curiosity."

"Not that you have any of your own."

Kirsten hurried to the hall phone, aware that Rose and Frank were straining to hear every word.

For long minutes she listened as the voice on the other end affirmed what the letter had stated. It was all a dream, she thought. This couldn't be happening to her. She'd never won anything of value in her life.

"And you're certain you've notified the right person?"

"Miss Kirsten Stevens, 345 Elm, Fairfield, Ohio," the voice intoned. "You're the grand prize winner. A first-class round-trip ticket to Maurab. A room at the plush Mediterranean Villa, complete with meals, tips and transportation to and from the airport. Your prize must be claimed within two months. When you notify us of the date you've chosen, your tickets and further information will be in the mail."

"Thank you."

Dazed, Kirsten floated back to the kitchen. Rose and Frank watched her. Slowly her look of surprise was replaced by a dazzling smile. "I really am the winner. No strings attached."

"Oh, Kirsten." The elderly couple hurried around the table to hug her.

Amy, caught up in their enthusiasm, climbed on Kirsten's lap. "Are you going away now?"

"Not so soon," she said with a laugh. "But I do have to claim my prize within two months." She bit her lip. "Spring break starts at the end of the month. I promised to house-sit for Dr. Briggs and his wife while they're in Florida. I wonder if one of the other teachers can take the job?"

"Of course they can," Rose insisted, returning to her nearly forgotten dinner. "Wait till they hear you're going to Maurab."

"Where's that?" Amy asked, still clinging to Kirsten's neck.

"It's a little country on the other side of the world," Kirsten murmured. Recalling her geography lessons, she added, "It's nestled in the foothills of the Alps. A small, prosperous kingdom lying like a sparkling jewel beside the Mediterranean. At least that's what my textbook said."

"Kingdom." The little girl singled out the most interesting word. "Is there a king and queen?"

Kirsten thought a minute. "The queen died a few years ago. There is a king, though. And a beautiful palace."

Turning to her grandmother, the little girl shrieked, "Wait till the king sees Kirsten. He'll kiss her, and she'll wake up, and they'll live happily ever after."

Everyone laughed.

"I think you have your stories mixed up a bit," Kirsten said gently. "That's Sleeping Beauty. Besides," she added softly, "the king is probably quite old. Old enough to be my father."

"Does that mean you can't be queen?"

Kirsten kissed her cheek. "That only happens in fairy tales. But I'm still going to have a wonderful time." She turned to Rose. "If you don't mind, I think I'll go up to my room. I couldn't possibly eat now. There's too much to plan."

Rose nodded her understanding. "What will the temperature be like in Maurab?"

"Warm," Kirsten called, heading for the stairs. "In Maurab, it's always summertime."

As the plane dropped below the clouds, Kirsten strained for her first glimpse of Maurab. The tiny principality, she'd read in her guidebook, was named for the mountain that loomed like a fortress on its border: Mount Maurab. As they circled lower, Kirsten noted the brilliant turquoise waters of the Mediterranean. White sandy beaches sparkled in the sunshine. Every harbor seemed crowded with yachts and sailing vessels flying the flags of foreign countries. The gently rolling countryside was dotted with colorful villas and sprawling hotels. When the plane tipped its wings, Kirsten caught sight of the palace, perched at the top of rock-strewn cliffs. With a roar of engines, the plane touched down.

A few years ago Kirsten had accompanied her class on a school outing to an amusement park. In a moment of weakness she'd been persuaded to ride the roller coaster. After experiencing terror and fascination, she was left with a feeling of numbness. Now she experienced the same sense of disorientation as she stood on legs of rubber and reached for her travel bag. This wasn't really happening to her. It seemed like a dream. A wonderful dream. Following the crowd along the center aisle of the plane, she shed her winter coat and stepped out into brilliant sunshine.

In the airport a uniformed driver held a sign emblazoned with her name. After fetching her luggage from the carrousel, he settled her comfortably in the hotel limousine, and they sped away.

The narrow highway wound its way among pink-walled villas and exotic, tile-roofed houses. The countryside was a riot of blazing flowers. Scarlet hibiscus, salmon-hued bougainvillea and delicate white gardenias were as abundant as the wild daisies that dotted her beloved Ohio fields in summer.

The hotel was an ornate marble-and-tile building overlooking the sea. An open courtyard connected smaller, low buildings with the lobby and restaurants. From the main building, Kirsten was driven in a covered electric cart to a private cottage. Beneath an orange tiled roof, walls of vine-covered stucco offered a lush welcome. Drawing open all the drapes, Kirsten looked out on a vista of white sand and cool blue ocean. After disposing of the luggage, the bellman showed her how to obtain service at a moment's notice with the simple touch of a button, then led her to the private screened patio and pool. The air was heavy with the fragrance of exotic flowers.

When she was alone, she slipped out of her shoes and allowed her feet to sink into the thick carpet. With a little sigh of pleasure, she began slowly walking through the luxurious rooms, too dazed to take it all in at once. She was here. Really here in Maurab.

Laughing, she sank down on the edge of the king-size bed. Feeling the soft mattress, she fell back and gave a sigh of pure pleasure. For two whole weeks, she could live the kind of life she'd always dreamed of. Still smiling, she closed her eyes. What had Amy whispered when she'd kissed her goodbye? "I just know you're going to meet a handsome king. And I'll come visit you in the palace."

Clasping her hands behind her head, Kirsten stared at the ornate ceiling. She was too old to believe in fairy tales. Besides, her life was a good one. She'd been lucky enough to find a room with the Johnsons, who treated her like one of the family. And she had a job she loved.

Her lids fluttered. Still, every girl dreamed of meeting a handsome prince and living happily ever after.

She sat up and smoothed down the jacket of her suit. She'd been listening to Amy too long. She'd have to be content with two weeks of doing exactly as she pleased, in the prettiest country she'd ever seen. Her practical nature told her that was enough for anyone.

Still, she thought, dancing across the room and stepping onto the sun-warmed stones of the private terrace, it was tempting to daydream. With a shake of her head, Kirsten hurried inside to change into her bathing suit. She'd save the dreaming for later. Right now, she was going to bask in the luxury of swimming in her own personal pool.

Kirsten slipped out of her sandals before stepping onto the sandy beach. Despite the darkness, the sand still held the warmth of afternoon. She fought a vague feeling of restlessness. The nap she'd taken before dinner had upset her internal clock. A walk along the deserted beach was just what she needed.

Dinner in the hotel's gourmet dining room had been a wonderful experience. The maître d' had escorted her to a table overlooking the harbor, where she could watch the play of ships' lights across the darkening water. While she sipped red wine and feasted on beef burgundy, she had enjoyed the parade of elegant men and women. Some had just arrived, sleek and tanned, aboard their yachts. Others, she was certain, lived in the pink-walled villas scattered along the hillsides. There was an aura of wealth and sophistication about them. And some, with cameras around their necks, were tourists, sporting sunburns and wearing comfortable shoes. All of them, Kirsten decided, looked as if they somehow belonged in this life of opulence.

The breeze off the ocean lifted the hem of her sundress. Shivering slightly, she stepped up on a rock and stared out to sea.

The dog growled low in his throat. The man beside him touched a hand to his head to quiet him, then lifted narrowed eyes to study the apparition on the rock.

Beautiful enough to be a mermaid. But this one had legs. Great legs. In the darkness, the white sundress and waist-length golden hair held him spellbound. He glanced at the sandals she held in one hand, then studied her profile: the lush sweep of lashes, the small, upturned nose and firm chin. His gaze skimmed downward to the high breasts, the tiny waist and rounded hips, the bare feet beneath the drift of white gown.

Sensing someone watching her, the vision turned. With a little gasp, she scrambled from the rock. The man walked closer. Obediently the dog heeled.

The man was tall, well over six feet. Despite his dark clothing, it was obvious that he had the trim build of an athlete. His features were obscured by the darkness. All she could make out were gleaming white teeth and strange, compelling eyes.

In his hand the glowing tip of a cigarette illuminated the darkness. The exotic scent of sweet Turkish tobacco enveloped him.

She had to lift her head to speak to him. When she did, her hair spilled over one bare shoulder, leaving the other pale and luminous in the moonlight.

"I hope your dog is friendly." Her voice, with its husky, slightly breathless quality, intrigued him.

"Only when I tell him to be." His tone was low, cultured, with a slight accent. She could hear the smile in it. "Don't worry. I've already warned him to behave."

"Good."

He sensed the relief in that single word. "You're a visitor in my country. American?"

She nodded.

"Your first visit?" He found himself entranced by the silken hair that kissed her cheeks as she nodded her head. Up close he inhaled the fragrance of her perfume, a delicate, ethereal scent that pulled at him. "What do you think of it?"

A smile touched her lips, lit her eyes. "It's beautiful. Like a dream."

"Where are you staying?"

"At the Villa."

In the shadows, she saw his lips curve. "One of our best. It has old-world charm. Much nicer than the newer hotels."

"When I saw the cottage I'm staying in, I fell in love with it. And imagine, my own exclusive pool."

"The staff is trained to guard their guests' privacy. Your next-door neighbor could be royalty or a head of state, but you would never know."

He enjoyed the way her eyebrows lifted at his words. A dreamy smile softened her features. "How exciting."

As a breeze tossed her hair, he saw her shiver. "You should have brought a wrap. The night air gets quite cool. Here, use my jacket."

Seeing the way his gaze lingered on her bare shoulders, she felt her heart thud in her chest and took a step away. "I should go back."

As she turned, she spotted the silhouette of a man on the hill above the beach. Alongside him stood a second figure. Both were watching her intently. Or was it the man beside her who held their interest?

She turned back and touched his arm. Beside him, the dog gave a warning growl, and she snatched her hand away.

"Are you in some sort of trouble?" Out of the corner of her eye, she thought she saw one of the figures lift something to his shoulder. A rifle? Her heart leaped to her throat.

She'd felt the stranger stiffen at her touch. Now, with a word of warning to the animal, he looked down into her frightened eyes. "What do you mean?"

She nodded toward the two figures at the top of the hill. Her voice lowered. "I think those men are watching you."

Warmth—or humor—softened his tone. "Don't worry. I'm fine. It's you. They're probably admiring your beauty."

She took a hesitant step back, then looked up. In that brief instant, she saw his eyes, cool and catlike in the moonlight. There was no fear in him, she realized. Instead he had an air of confidence. And something more. Power. Raw power.

— "Well." She licked her lips, and felt his gaze move to her mouth. "If you're certain."

"I'm absolutely certain. I don't want you to waste one precious moment of your visit to my country worrying about me, Miss..."

"Stevens. Kirsten Stevens."

"Kirsten." When he repeated her name, she realized she'd never heard it sound so beautiful. "Here, Kirsten. You're trembling."

He wrapped his jacket around her shoulders, allowing his hands to linger on them a moment. The softness of her skin jolted him, reminding him of finest silk. Slowly he drew the lapels together, all the while staring down into her wide, startled eyes.

Snugly encased in his jacket, she was acutely aware of the masculine scents surrounding her: leather, tobacco, a decidedly musky, male fragrance that assaulted her senses.

If she'd followed through on her initial intention to run away, she could have been spared this encounter. Now he was touching her, and his touch caused her strange, unsettling feelings. She felt a sudden, gnawing fear. This man was too sure of himself, too bold. He was, she knew instinctively, a man accustomed to having what he wanted.

She tried to draw away, but his hands held her fast.

She cloaked her fear in anger. "If you don't let me go, I'll..."

"Scream?"

She heard the laughter in his tone and resented it. "Yes. And those men . . ."

"Will be forced to come even closer to investigate the lady in distress."

He saw her gaze flit toward the figures on the hill, then back to him.

As much as she wanted to flee, she hoped she could do so quietly, without a scene, without drawing undue attention to herself. There was something about those dark figures watching them that disturbed her.

While he continued to hold the lapels of his jacket about her, he drew her slightly closer. The warmth of his body engulfed her. She saw his gaze focus on her mouth. He intended to kiss her.

Her throat went dry. He watched her eyes widen slightly as he bent toward her, drawing her inexorably nearer.

Her heart seemed to stop. "I don't . . ."

His lips covered hers in the softest, lightest kiss she'd ever experienced.

The rest of her words died in her throat. She couldn't even remember what she'd been saying.

His lips were warm. Warm and firm. But he exerted no pressure, demanded nothing more than the touch of her lips in return. The kiss was gentle. So gentle that she might have imagined it if it weren't for the tremors that rocked her.

This couldn't be happening. This sort of thing didn't happen between total strangers. Her blood shouldn't flow like molten lava. Her heart shouldn't race and tumble in her breast. Her knees shouldn't grow weak and threaten to buckle. Her mind shouldn't whirl and swirl in a hazy cloud of soft white cotton.

When he lifted his head, she felt dizzy, light-headed. Afraid she'd fall, she steadied herself by clutching blindly at his waist. When she looked up into his eyes, they were narrow, amber slits, studying her as if in amazement.

Feeling the stunning impact of that single kiss, he took a halting step backward.

She swung back her hand in an arc, bringing her palm up. He caught it easily and held it in an iron grip. "Too predictable," he whispered. Again, she heard the thread of humor. "You should have thought of something more original."

Furious, she stared up into laughing eyes. While she watched, his smile faded. Slowly, seductively, his head lowered. He was going to kiss her again. She swallowed, feeling her heart leap to her throat. She couldn't permit it. Her legs were already rubber, her knees too weak to support her. If she allowed him the simplest touch, the briefest of kisses, she'd lose her last shred of dignity.

Afraid, she managed a step backward, away from his touch. As if in a daze, he lifted his head.

Her breath trembled through parted lips as she struggled to compose herself. This is madness, she thought. Her throat felt parched. She was surprised at how difficult it was to speak. "I have to go." To hide her shame at her uncharacteristic behavior, she stiffened her spine. Her chin jutted defiantly. It was, after all, only a kiss.

He felt her warm breath caress his face. "Good night, Kirsten Stevens. We will meet again."

Angry at the laughter in his tone, she turned and fled along the beach, her forgotten sandals still clutched absently in one hand.

We will meet again. Not a question, a statement. She shivered, but it wasn't from the ocean breeze. She had no need to turn around. She could feel the stranger's eyes, cool and amber, watching her. Two other men, she knew, were watching her as well. Despite his protests, she sensed that they weren't simply casual observers.

What had happened to her common sense? In her hometown, it never would have occurred to her to allow a stranger to touch her, let alone kiss her. It was the long flight, she told herself, and this exotic setting—a moon-drenched beach on a foreign shore. For one wild moment, she'd been carried away by the romance of it all.

She would have to be more careful. No more midnight strolls on deserted beaches. No more encounters with strangers. She'd almost stumbled into something over her head.

Chapter Two

Kirsten lay bathed in a pool of sunlight. Outside her window a chorus of birds trilled. The heavenly fragrance of gardenias filled the room. She stretched, loving the feel of the cool sheets against her naked skin. Paradise. This morning, she'd awakened in paradise.

She'd fallen asleep last night with a vague premonition of danger. That man on the beach had stirred something in her. She'd sensed such strength, such power in him. And those men watching him. She let out a little laugh of surprise. In the darkness, she'd actually convinced herself that she'd seen a gun. Her imagination was running wild. Next, she'd be thinking he was a cat burglar, or a jewel thief, and those men were some sort of international police. She sat up, her heart racing at the thought. Preposterous. She was letting the romance of this little kingdom get to her.

She had run off wearing the stranger's jacket. A thorough examination had revealed no clues to its owner's identity. The pockets were empty. The label declared that the jacket had been custom-made in Paris. The fabric was expensive. It was obvious the man had excellent taste.

Last night she'd decided she wouldn't worry about returning it. He knew where she was staying. He'd certainly come looking for it. She would leave it at the hotel desk later today.

She tossed back the sheet and strode across the room. After ordering breakfast, Kirsten tied on her bikini and dived into the pool. Taking slow, measured strokes, she swam the length, touched the edge, then dipped below the water and glided to the far side. Back and forth she swam, feeling her body respond to the demands she made.

Floating on her back, she stared at the clouds. When she was little, she'd wanted to fly like the birds. Her father, a pilot, often took her up in his plane. At those times she'd experienced an exhilarating sense of freedom. Her mother, a dancer who modeled occasionally, used to take her tiny daughter with her on assignments or to her dance classes. Hers was a childhood filled with love, adventure and security. The idyll ended one rainy Sunday. Returning from a weekend in Chicago, the plane her father was piloting crashed. Her parents were killed instantly. Nine-year-old Kirsten was pulled from the wreckage. In a state of shock, she'd retreated into a protective shell, unable to do the simplest things. The doctors did what they could. But it was Gram, her father's mother, who had turned Kirsten's life around.

Gram called herself a tough old bird. It was an apt description. Until her stroke at the age of seventy-two, she'd piloted her own plane, driven a tractor as well as a motorcycle, run the farm with the help of two boarders and made it all look like fun. When her frightened, grieving granddaughter had come to live with her, Gram had refused to pamper her. Giving her love, direction and guidance, but adamantly refusing to do for her what she could do for herself, Gram had taught the little girl how to live all over again. She had expected Kirsten to do all the things the other children in the town did. In time, Kirsten had done them better.

Pulling herself from the pool, Kirsten wrung the water from her hair. What would her life have been like if the accident hadn't occurred? Would life have continued to be one grand and glorious adventure? Tossing her head in anger, she picked up a towel. It was foolish to speculate about what might have been. The fact was, she reminded herself sternly, everyone had to cope with some hardship in life. What had Gram always said? Sometimes it was necessary to accept fate gracefully and get on with living. Kirsten smiled. She could still hear that dear old staccato voice admonishing her to stop feeling sorry for herself and get back to work.

Patting herself dry, she draped the towel about herself like a sarong. In the sumptuous gold-and-white bedroom, she brushed her hair until it fell in soft waves down her back. At the sound of a knock, she removed her wet suit and slipped into an ivory silk kimono before padding barefoot to the door.

"Good morning, miss," the waiter said in slightly accented English.

"Good morning. Can you bring that to the patio, please?"

He followed her, and began silently setting breakfast for two on the round glass table.

"I'm afraid you've brought the wrong order," she said, staring in dismay at the assortment of dishes.

He glanced down and read his instructions. Looking up, he added with a knowing smile, "It has all been arranged." His smile grew. "I know you will enjoy."

Bowing discreetly, he backed from the terrace and let himself out. Kirsten was on her way to the phone when she heard a slight sound on the patio. Turning, she found herself staring into the tawny eyes of the man from the beach.

Last night he had been hidden in shadow. Now she was free to study the thick, dark hair, cut very short, that framed an extraordinarily handsome face. Dark brows arched over his eyes, which, in dazzling sunlight, were molten gold. He had high, aristocratic cheekbones, a finely sculpted nose and lips that were full and sensual.

"I believe you have something of mine."

Uncomfortably aware of his scrutiny, she turned and retrieved the jacket from her bedroom. "I'm sorry. I didn't realize I still had it on until it was too late."

"Don't be sorry. It gave me an excuse to see you again. You will join me for breakfast?" She heard the warmth of laughter in his voice.

The truth dawned. "You ordered this." Without waiting for his response, she added, "May I remind you that this is my room?"

A smile touched the corners of his lips. "I'm sure that my action seems bold to an independent American woman like you. But I assure you, it was all arranged discreetly." At the frosty look in her eyes, he brought his hand to reveal a perfect gardenia. "I had to pick this. It reminded me of you." His gaze slid over her fine blond hair and the creamy skin visible beneath her silk wrap.

Stepping closer, he tucked the flower behind her ear. He felt a sudden jolt as the back of his knuckles brushed her hair. All night the taste of her had lingered on his lips. Sleep had eluded him. For the hundredth time, he wondered if he'd only imagined the feelings that had pulsed between them. He'd had no choice but to find her.

"I've always had a weakness for cool blondes."

"And I've always had a weakness for breakfast, as long as I don't have to make it. No matter whom," she added dryly, "I'm forced to share it with."

He threw back his head and laughed. "The blonde is not so cool, I see. I like a woman with a temper."

"I'm not interested in what you like." Before she could sit down, he was beside her, holding her chair. Looking up she added, "I don't even know your name."

"Forgive me." He caught her hand in his and stared down into her eyes. "My friends call me Stefan."

Kirsten expected him to shake her hand. Instead he lifted her hand to his mouth and brushed his lips lightly over the back of her fingers. Tiny pinpricks of pleasure shot along her arm. Stunned, she could only stare at him while he gave her a bemused smile.

It pleased him that he'd caught her off guard. "May I join you for breakfast?"

She motioned with her free hand. "I suppose, since you went to all this trouble." An impish grin fought with her frown. "It would be a shame to waste it."

As she poured coffee from a silver urn, she asked, "Are you staying at the villa, too?"

"No." He sipped and, expertly sidestepping her question, said, "Excellent coffee."

She lifted a silver dome to reveal Eggs Benedict, poached salmon and crisp points of rye toast. Stefan watched as she took a tentative bite. He relaxed visibly when she sighed, "Oh, this is heavenly. A meal fit for a king."

"I'm glad you like it. I wasn't sure what you usually had for breakfast."

"What I usually have," she said, taking a second bite and savoring it, "is black coffee on the run. On weekends, when I have more time, I have a bowl of cereal."

"And where is it you run to?" He found himself fascinated with her beautiful face and its flawless complexion, completely free of makeup. Her perfectly formed eyebrows were the same pale blond as the hair that streamed down her back. Her cheekbones were the sort models would die for. Her skin was flushed with just a hint of sun. Her lips, unadorned, were made for kissing. The thought tormented him.

"I teach school," she said, lifting her coffee cup. "Second grade."

"Do you like it?"

He saw the smile that lit her eyes and softened all her features. "I'm crazy about my kids. Every year there's a new challenge."

"And you don't back away from challenges?"

She laughed, a rich, husky sound. "Isn't that what life's all about?"

He regarded her a moment. "Yes." His voice lowered thoughtfully. "Yes. Life is about challenges." Propping his chin on his hand, he stared at her across the table.

She mimicked him, and he reached across and caught her fingers, intertwining hers with his.

"Tell me about yourself. What are your parents like?"

He felt her fingers tighten in his. "They're both dead. I was raised by my grandmother."

"And what does she do?"

"She was a farmer."

Was. He heard the pain in that single word.

"She died several years ago."

But, he guessed, this cool, self-assured woman missed her still. He could understand her sense of loss. "Any brothers or sisters?"

She shook her head. "What about you? Tell me about your family."

He smiled, and she was struck again by how appealing this arrogant man was when he relaxed.

"I have a father. He likes to appear very stern. But in truth, he's a pushover. He used to send for my mother if I had so much as a loose tooth. He gets misty eyed at the opera. Ever since my mother died, he's become very protective of all of us. Especially my younger sister."

"Tell me about her."

He warmed to his subject. "Alana is beautiful. She's in her last year at the Sorbonne. Very bright. Too sensitive, though. Whenever she hears criticism of herself or the family, she feels crushed."

"Why would anyone want to criticize your family?"

He shrugged, choosing to ignore the question. "Then there are my brothers. Andrew is only a year younger than I, but I play the role of older brother to the limit. He hates it. We're very competitive. I graduated from Harvard the year before he did. That gives me the right to expect a certain amount of respect from a kid brother." For a brief moment, Stefan's voice lost its humor. "The truth is, I'd gladly step aside and let him take my place for a while. But it isn't possible." He brightened. "And then there's the youngest, Michael. He's seventeen. Discovering cars and girls, and making passable grades in school."

"It sounds like you have a very loving family."

He nodded. "Of necessity, we've always been close."

Kirsten sensed a sadness in him. Abruptly he changed the subject. "Enough about me. What kind of music do you like?"

Music? Were his moods always so mercurial? She thought a moment. "All kinds, I guess. Classical. Old forties and fifties. Rock. Country. What about you?"

"The same. My sister insists that I have no musical taste. When I'm trying to impress someone, I just say I have eclectic taste."

"Very clever. I'll have to remember that." She could feel the tremors his touch was causing. Her cheeks were growing hotter by the minute. "Stefan." She swallowed and met his direct gaze. "I need my hand back." At his questioning look, she added, "To finish my breakfast."

"Ah. A fair enough request. I did promise to feed you, didn't I?" He watched as she enjoyed the delicious meal. "What about art? Do you have any favorite artists?"

From anyone else, these questions would have seemed intrusive. From Stefan, they only seemed signs of his inquisitive mind.

"Are you asking if I collect them?" She laughed. "Not on a teacher's salary. But I do have favorites. Gauguin. Any of the French Impressionist painters. And I can't forget American artists. Wyeth especially. I studied art, hoping to paint. I finally had to admit I'd only be a Sunday painter. I'm not very good." She gave a self-conscious laugh, and for a moment lowered her lashes. It seemed incredible that she was willing to reveal so much of herself to this stranger.

He was staring at her so intently that she felt herself growing warm. "I knew. Last night on the beach," he murmured almost to himself, "I knew so many things about you without even asking. And I knew you would fascinate me."

"The same lack of taste," she said dryly.

They shared a knowing laugh.

She glanced down, avoiding his eyes. "Are you going to tell me which artists you admire?"

"Better than that. Someday I'll show you." His smile grew. "Do you sail?"

She was caught off guard by the sudden change of topic. "Not very well. But I can stay afloat if we tip."

"We won't tip over. You can trust me."

For some reason she didn't care to explore further; she believed him.

He stood, without having eaten a bite. "Can you be ready in an hour?"

"For what?"

"I want to take you sailing. Will you join me?"

Kirsten dismissed the tiny fears fluttering in her stomach. He was, after all, still very much a stranger. Yet she had to admit that she wanted to go sailing with him. He was fascinating. "I suppose so. Yes, I'd like that." Pushing back her chair, she prepared to see him to the door of her cottage. Instead, he strode toward the low brick wall that enclosed her patio.

"Where are you going?"

"Out the way I came."

"Stefan." She moved closer and gave him a long look. "Are you avoiding someone? Are those men still following you?"

He caught a strand of her hair and lifted it, watching it sift through his fingers. Meeting her gaze, he murmured, "You had them so dazzled, they forgot about me."

"Stop teasing." Her voice lowered. "I'm worried about you. Are you in some kind of trouble?"

His hand dropped to her shoulder. He could feel her delicate bones beneath the fine fabric. "So small and slender," he murmured. "Do you think you could protect me from danger?"

"I don't think that's funny. If you're in trouble, you should go to the police."

"Trust me, Kirsten. There's nothing wrong." Both his hands clutched her shoulders firmly. He drew her close, and his voice dropped to a whisper. "If I ever do find myself in trouble, though, I think I'd like you on my side."

His gaze focused on her mouth. He was mesmerized by the sight of those lips, warm and parted, and only inches from his. One movement. He needed only to lower his head, to brush his lips over hers, and he would feel the passion he'd discovered last night.

She was so small. Her perfectly sculpted body was quite visible beneath her silk wrap. He thought about pressing her against him and felt a sudden jolt of desire, swift and powerful.

Kirsten watched the play of emotions on his face. Studying him closely, she had the feeling that she knew this man. She'd never met him before. That much was certain. She could never forget someone like him. But she knew him, knew about him. Somewhere, sometime, she had seen him—or his picture.

At her close scrutiny, he lifted an eyebrow. The expression gave him an aristocratic, almost aloof, bearing. He felt her stiffen slightly, and knew in that moment that she'd had a sudden flash of insight. He had wanted the charade to continue for a while longer. He'd been enjoying the anonymity. For so long, he'd yearned for someone he could really talk to. Her intelligence, her humor, even her cool treatment of him, filled a void. Now, his anonymity would end. With a pang of regret, he saw her eyes widen as knowledge of his identity slowly dawned.

In her research on the country, Kirsten had seen the outdated pictures. Ever since her arrival here she had seen the posters—in the hotel lobby, in almost every shop. Even the country's stamps bore the portrait of the Maurab royal family: the strikingly handsome king; his eldest son and wife, both of whom had died tragically a year ago, the three younger sons and daughter. Yes, she had indeed seen pictures of this man, though in the photographs he was not garbed in a casual oatmeal-colored sweater and cotton slacks, but dressed in a gold-braided military uniform. He was the eldest surviving son, the heir to the throne of Maurab.

Pushing herself fiercely from his arms, she cried, "Stefan. Of course. Stefan Larousse. Prince Stefan of Maurab."

He watched in silence as she backed away from him. As her shock slowly gave way to anger, her eyes danced with little points of flame. Her chin lifted defiantly. Hands on her hips, she released the fury that was building inside her.

"The prince of Maurab. Quite the playboy. I've seen your picture often enough, always taken at some disco or celebrity affair. You prefer petulant, dark-eyed daughters of dukes and counts, I believe. And an occasional actress." Her voice betrayed the pain beneath her shock and anger. "Why me? Was this all some kind of a cruel joke? Were you planning to see how long you could fool the little schoolteacher?"

Stefan took a step closer. Seeing the hurt look in her eyes, he winced. "I didn't intend it as a joke, Kirsten. I saw you on the beach last night and I was intrigued. I wanted to see you again. Is that such a crime?"

"You've embarrassed me. I feel...I feel cheated. You knew who I was. I told you everything you wanted to know. Like a silly fool, I answered all your impertinent questions. But I had no idea who you were."

His voice lowered. "It wasn't a game, Kirsten. It was simply a way of protecting myself. I wanted you to know me, to trust me first."

"Trust." He saw the outrage in her eyes. "You betrayed my trust."

Stefan kept his hands stiffly at his sides, careful not to touch her. "If I had introduced myself, would you have relaxed in my presence? Would you?" He stepped closer. "Can't you just see it? 'Hello, I'm Prince Stefan of Maurab. I'd like to send my car around to take you to breakfast at the palace.'" He stared down at her. "Would you have come?"

Kirsten bit her lip. What he said made sense. She never would have agreed to have breakfast with royalty. The very thought was ludicrous. Yet until she'd discovered who he was, this morning had seemed like a wonderful, carefree holiday. She felt the twinge of regret. Now everything was spoiled.

"I did intend to tell you. In time." He brushed a strand of hair from her cheek and stared down into her eyes. "But I wanted to go slowly. I wanted to get to know you. I wanted you to have time to know me." His voice hardened slightly. "Not the prince of Maurab. Me." With a finger beneath her chin, he lifted her face gently. "Can you understand that?"

When she refused to answer, he whispered, "Am I forgiven?"

- Kirsten hesitated, still feeling the sting of humiliation. Staring into those cool amber eyes, she sensed his sincerity. Swallowing back the angry words she'd been about to utter, she nodded her head slightly.

She heard him slowly expel his breath.

A sudden thought made her lips curl at the corners. "Those men on the hill. They were bodyguards?"

Stefan nodded.

Her smile turned into a chuckle. "I'd already decided you were an international jewel thief. I thought they were watching you to catch you when you turned over the spoils of your latest heist."

He threw back his head and roared. "I'm sorry to disappoint you. Of course, I could help myself to a handful of the royal jewels. Would that satisfy you?" Seeing her smile, he pressed his advantage. "My invitation still stands. I'd like to take you sailing today."

"On your yacht?" she asked sarcastically.

"On my small, two-passenger sailboat." He ran the collar of her kimono between his thumb and forefinger, toying with the fabric.

Kirsten felt a tiny thrill of pleasure at his light touch. Glancing up, she saw his eyes narrow slightly. Had he felt it, too? His expression gave nothing away.

"I'd like that. As long as you don't dump me in the ocean."

"You're in good hands." He ran his hands lightly over the tops of her silk-clad arms and remembered the way she had felt pressed against him last night. He'd been stunned by the passions unleashed by their simple kiss. He was hungry for more of the same. As his gaze centered on her mouth, he saw her stiffen. She was already withdrawing from him. It was something he'd always had trouble dealing with. Strangers who were completely relaxed in his presence suddenly became stiff and formal when they realized his position.

He dropped his hands to his sides and stepped away. "Be ready in an hour."

"Make it two. I have some postcards to write."

As he walked across the patio, she called, "Why don't you use the door?"

"My men are just beyond this hedge. I wouldn't want to make them crazy."

"Will they be sailing with us?" He saw the sudden look of alarm in her eyes.

"There's only room for two. But they'll be close. They're never far from me."

He stepped over the low brick wall. As he moved away, she saw two shadows fall into step behind him.

Kirsten pressed a trembling hand to her throat. The prince. The heir to the throne of Maurab. Here in her room.

Taking the gardenia from behind her ear, she absently inhaled the sweet perfume.

While she showered and dressed and tried to write clever postcards to her friends at home, the image of Stefan intruded, ruining her concentration.

This didn't happen to farm-bred schoolteachers from the Midwest. They never even got to meet a member of royalty, let alone go sailing with one of them. This wasn't really happening to her. When she finally came down to earth, she was going to land with a thud.

But as long as she was dreaming, she thought, hurriedly going through the clothes in her closet, she was going to enjoy every glorious minute of it.

Chapter Three

Kirsten watched the tall figure stride up the path toward her cottage, and felt her heart miss a beat. Sunlight glistened on dark hair still damp from the shower. He was wearing shorts and a white knit shirt that revealed tanned, muscular limbs. On his feet were white boating shoes.

For a moment, she felt a wave of panic. He's a prince, her mind warned. He's playing some sort of silly game with you. After all the glamorous, sophisticated women he's known, how can he find a simple schoolteacher from Ohio interesting? Ever since he'd left, she'd been carrying on this same argument. In college, Kirsten had watched her friends fall in and out of love. Even now, some of the young teachers managed to find a summer romance each time school ended. But she wasn't interested in a fling. Kirsten prided herself on her practicality. She didn't believe in love at first sight. Especially with a prince.

He's a man, her heart reminded her, recalling their shared moonlight kiss. A man, with a man's passions, a man's dreams. Still, she wasn't about to lose her head—or her heart—to this man.

At his knock on the door, she forgot her nervousness. This was a chance to spend a day sailing on the blue Mediterranean, to glimpse a life-style beyond her narrow world. Nothing more.

"Did I give you enough time to finish your postcards?" he asked as she pulled open the door.

"Just enough." She indicated the littered writing desk. "I'll drop them in the lobby on my way out."

"We won't be leaving through the lobby. I'll give them to LeClerc. He'll see to them."

"LeClerc?"

"One of my men." He gave her a slow appraisal. She had fashioned her long hair into a fat braid, which fell over one shoulder. Over simple khaki shorts she wore a bright red blouse, tied at the midriff.

He said softly, "Maurab is fortunate to have you as a guest, Kirsten Stevens. You are beautiful."

She resented the flush that stole up her throat and colored her cheeks. She was behaving like a silly schoolgirl.

He looked wonderful, too. But, she decided, she'd keep that thought to herself. He'd probably grown up hearing how handsome, talented and perfectly groomed he was. She had no intention of feeding his ego further.

Taking her hand, he led her along the flower-strewn walk. The breeze carried the scent of hundreds of exotic blooms.

His car was a sleek black Ferrari. After settling her inside, he slid behind the wheel.

"You drive yourself?"

He flashed her a warm smile. "Since I was sixteen, as a matter of fact."

"I just thought you'd have a chauffeur."

"Disappointed?"

She shook her head. "Pleasantly surprised."

As she glanced over her shoulder, she saw a high-powered black car following closely.

"Your men?"

He looked in the rearview mirror and nodded.

Her pleasure faded slightly. It was impossible to forget who this man was. The reminders were everywhere. "Will they sail alongside us, too?"

He gave her a gentle smile. "At times. Especially if any other boats get too close. But most of the time they'll maintain a discreet distance."

They drove along a picture-perfect harbor where dozens of boats tugged at their moorings. Stefan turned into a circular drive and pulled up to a pink-stucco building whose walls were dotted with ivy. An attendant opened their doors, then drove the Ferrari to a private parking space. Taking her arm, Stefan led Kirsten along the dock to a sleek white and teak sailboat. As they approached, two men stepped from the boat and stood aside as Stefan helped Kirsten aboard. As she turned her head, Kirsten saw one of the men nod his head slightly. Glancing at Stefan, she saw his almost imperceptible acknowledgment.

"More of your men?"

He nodded.

"Just to stand guard over a boat?"

"To check the safety of the craft before we leave the dock."

Safety. He spoke the word casually, as if it meant nothing. Kirsten shivered.

Starting the engine, Stefan maneuvered the boat out of the slip and through the shallows of the harbor. Seated beside him, Kirsten felt the fresh breeze as they picked up speed. Above them, a cloudless sky promised a perfect day on the water.

She turned her head to watch the play of Stefan's muscles as he manned the tiller. Along the back of his hand and up his arm dark hair glistened against deeply tanned skin. She thought of his hands touching her, holding her and felt a shocking tremor of desire.

"Cold?"

"No." She drew her gaze up to his face. "This sun is wonderful."

He loved the way she looked in the sunlight, all white skin and golden hair. A goddess. An untouched, untouchable goddess. As a strand of her hair whispered across his face, desire slammed into him like a fist.

Once they were in open water, he cut the engines and began hoisting the sails.

"You sit here, out of the way," Stefan said, indicating a cushioned area at the prow. "I don't want you to get hit in the head by the boom."

"I didn't come along to sit and watch. I want to help."

"It's going to require a little muscle for a while. This wind is tricky."

"Try me."

He shrugged. "Take this line. When I order it up, pull with all your might. When my line is free, I'll help you."

Kirsten smiled to herself. Stefan thought he was dealing with a helpless little kitten. She wondered what her baseball and track teams would think of that appraisal.

She watched in fascination as Stefan pulled his shirt over his head, revealing a back and chest corded with muscles. Sweat beaded his forehead and chest and ran in little rivulets along the hollow of his lower back.

"All right. Pull."

Heaving in the taut line, Kirsten pulled with all her might and felt the sail slowly unfurl and billow in the wind. After securing his own line, Stefan reached his arms around her to grasp her rope. With his hands just above hers, they managed to secure the final sail.

"I'm impressed," he said, chuckling against her ear. "Your looks are deceiving. I didn't think you were strong enough to manage that sail."

"Let that be a warning," she said, with a laugh, turning in his arms. "Get fresh with me and I'll be forced to show you my left hook."

"It might be worth it," he muttered, fighting the need to draw her even closer against him. "If you could read my mind, you'd probably show me your defense techniques right now."

"Watch it, Stefan."

"I'm warned. Here." He patted the bench. "Take the tiller for a minute." When he had secured all the lines, he settled himself beside her and murmured, "I hope you like speed. This is a day made for flying over the waves."

With one hand firmly on the tiller and the other around her shoulders, Stefan directed the little boat with great skill. The strong breeze tore at their backs and whipped their hair. Salty spray lashed their faces, leaving them laughing and breathless.

"You didn't need another bath," Stefan murmured, wiping Kirsten's face with a handkerchief.

"The water feels good in this hot sun."

Without warning he dipped his mouth to a droplet of water that beaded her temple. His unexpected action surprised both of them. Staring down into her wide eyes, he lowered his mouth to her cheek, then followed a salty trail to the corner of her lips. Heat, searing white heat, shot through her, leaving her dazed.

The boat tipped precariously.

Looking up sharply, Stefan turned the boat into the wind, avoiding disaster.

"I'd better keep my mind on the job at hand," he muttered with a wry smile.

For nearly two hours they skimmed the water, following the whims of the wind.

"How about lunch?" Stefan asked.

"I'd love it. Where will we go?"

He pointed. "See that deserted stretch of beach? Let's make for it."

"Will a magic genie suddenly appear with our food?"

"He already has." Lifting a canvas cover, Stefan revealed a hamper.

"I know you weren't up early this morning fixing all this."

He grinned. "Watch those mutinous mutterings. For all you know, I might be the world's greatest cook. Now get set to assist your captain."

Straining against the lines, they managed to lower the sails so that the boat glided in toward the white sand. When they were close enough to wade ashore, Stefan dropped anchor.

As they climbed over the side of the boat, Stefan scooped her in his arms and carried her ashore. Standing very still, he brushed her lips lightly with his.

At his questioning look, he muttered, "Just wanted to finish what we started back there, now that we're on solid ground."

But they weren't on solid ground at all, she realized. At the first touch of his lips, she felt her world tilting precariously. She strove to keep things light. "You forgot something."

He stared down at her.

"Lunch. The hamper is back in the boat. One of us is going to have to wade through the water again. And I think I'm looking at him."

Stefan chuckled and set her down. "If I weren't so hungry, I'd argue the point. But I was so dazzled by a certain beauty this morning, I forgot to eat breakfast."

As he walked away, Kirsten touched a finger to her lips. She could still feel the imprint of his lips on hers. No man's touch had ever had this effect on her.

In the shade of a tree, they spread their blanket. Lifting the lid of the hamper, Stefan began handing items to Kirsten. Giving a little laugh of pure delight, she shook her head in amazement. There was caviar and little crackers, along with wedges of sharp cheese. There was cold pheasant and sliced roast beef. Unwrapping another dish, she discovered brie, a delicately flavored soft cheese, and for dessert, perfect golden pears.

While she set out the food, Stefan uncorked a chilled bottle of champagne and poured two glasses.

Accepting one, she nibbled a cracker spread with caviar. "Your cook is very creative."

"Thank you."

"I'm not complimenting you. Don't pretend you did all this."

He chuckled and picked up a piece of cheese. "I'll admit I can't take the credit. We have a very efficient staff. But I did learn to cook when I attended Harvard. It was quite an experience."

"Are you good?"

"I didn't starve to death. Of course we did go out to dinner often. And we learned to exist on burgers and pizza."

"We. Did your bodyguards go with you to America?" Kirsten's gaze traveled to the small boat that hovered offshore. She had forgotten all about them until now.

"Only LeClerc. He had the apartment across the hall."

Leaning her back against a log, Kirsten studied the man who would be king. "What is it like?" she asked softly.

"What?"

"Life in a goldfish bowl. Knowing that wherever you go, someone is watching."

He shrugged expressively. "I suppose it must seem unbearable to someone who has known such freedom as you. But it's the only life I've ever known."

"But you lived in America. Surely you made friends, went to their apartments, saw how they lived."

He smiled gently. "But always I knew I would have to come back here and live my life." There was an underlying sadness in his tone. "I was lucky. For most of my years, I enjoyed a great deal of freedom. I attended schools in Europe and America, as did my younger brothers and sister. Except for a few personal attendants, I was free to experience the same things other people do." He glanced up, meeting her questioning look. His eyes, she noted, gleamed like a cat's in the sunlight. "You see, I wasn't raised to be king. That was for my older brother." His voice deepened with pain. "But now that he is gone, I have to accept my fate."

"You mean you wouldn't choose this life?"

He smiled gently. "Would anyone really choose his life? Would you? I would gladly trade places with one of my younger brothers. I enjoyed my childhood, knowing my older brother would have to assume responsibility for this country."

Stefan took a thin brown cigarette from his pocket. As he lit it, the air was filled with the pungent odor of tobacco.

"I'm afraid I learned this vice from my father," he said, watching the smoke curl above their heads. "When I was in your country, I smoked American cigarettes. Here at home, my father prefers Turkish tobacco. I've learned to like them."

Kirsten inhaled the aroma and was reminded of his jacket. The scent seemed a part of him.

"Do you ever have any privacy, real privacy?"

"I manage a little." He looked up. "Did you feel threatened by my men today?"

She shook her head, causing little tendrils of hair to drift softly about her face. "I never gave them a thought. We were too busy out there to think about anything else."

"But don't you see? That happens often. I must continue to live my life, even though there will always be men around to whom I have entrusted my safety."

Safety. That word again. She felt her heart lurch. "Why would anyone want to harm you?"

Shifting until he was seated beside her, he brushed a strand of hair from her eyes. "Let's talk of other things." His voice deepened. "Tell me, for instance, why I shouldn't kiss you."

"You're forgetting my right hook."

As she playfully balled her fist, he caught it in his hand and gently opened her fingers, pressing a kiss into her palm. Fire seemed to spread from her fingertips through her entire body. In one quick motion, he brought her down against the blanket. Surprised, she started to protest. His mouth covered hers, drowning out her cry.

He'd intended the kiss to be light and teasing. But the moment he touched her, everything changed. Though he lingered a moment, fighting to keep the kiss gentle, his need soon took over. Her delicate scent was enveloping him. Her breasts were flattened against his chest. Her soft, slender body yielded beneath his. His tongue expertly parted her lips and searched the moist secrets of her mouth.

Kirsten had intended to fight him. But the tenderness of his kiss caught her off guard. For a breathless moment she lay still, a feeling of helplessness sweeping over her. Warm sunlight filtered through the leaves of the tree, forming a kaleidoscope of light and color on her closed eyelids.

Under his guidance, her mouth became avid. Wrapping her arms around his waist, she drew him closer, needing to feel him against every part of her.

A seabird cried, and far out on the water a boat's horn sounded. The breeze fluttered the leaves of the tree, making a muted sound like lightly falling rain. Neither of them noticed. They were too caught up in needs that were shattering their control.

"I've thought of nothing but you since last night. I needed to kiss you again, to see if..."

His words trailed off as he brought his mouth down savagely on hers. Brilliant white lights blazed in her mind like a shower of stars. His mere kiss was causing feelings she'd never before experienced.

Chaos. Her mind whirled with disjointed thoughts and images. She couldn't seem to focus on a single thing. There was only the pleasure his lips brought. With a little sigh, she gave up trying to think and allowed herself the luxury of simply enjoying.

Drowning. He was drowning in the taste of her, the sweet, delicate scent of her. If he wasn't careful, he'd lose himself—step over the line of reason into the insanity that had hovered at the edges of his mind and taunted him all night.

Finally tearing his mouth from hers, Stefan pressed his lips to the little hollow at the base of her throat and heard her soft moan of pleasure. Opening his mouth, he ran his tongue along the delicate skin of her shoulder, and felt her shuddering response.

Desire pulsed within him. He wanted her as he'd never wanted anyone. He wanted to feel her warm and willing in his bed. He wanted to discover all the secret places of her body, to follow every line and curve, to make her ache for him the way he ached for her. No one had ever taken him so high with only a kiss.

"God, Kirsten, how lovely you are." He lifted his head to look at her.

Slowly, almost painfully, her lids fluttered open. Brilliant sunlight stabbed at her, causing her to blink in surprise. In his arms she had almost imagined herself cloaked in the private darkness of midnight.

"How can we—" She struggled to sit up, feeling disoriented. She'd responded to his touch, his kiss, the same way she'd responded last night. He seemed to uncover passions she'd never known she possessed.

But this wasn't just a man; he was a prince. Someday he would be king of this country.

Seeing the naked hunger in his eyes, she looked away. "It's time to leave, Stefan."

He ran his hands along her arms, feeling her shiver at his touch. There was no denying her response to him.

"I don't want to leave yet. We're alone here. Alone and free." Bringing his lips to her collarbone, he chuckled deep in his throat at her trembling reaction.

"Don't." She pulled away. She forced herself to stand on shaking legs. Shading her eyes from the sun, she stared at the boat still hovering offshore. "Alone? Of course. Just the two of us—and your men. Mustn't forget your bodyguards." Forcing herself from his grasp, she took several steps toward the beach. "I'm not interested in putting on a show for their enjoyment."

His voice lowered in anger. "Then we'll go to your villa. Is that private enough?"

"I guess I haven't made my message clear enough. No matter where we are, I'm not interested in your offer." With her hands on her hips, she hissed, "I'm not some love-starved little hick who's going to be dazzled by a titled playboy. Whatever it is you're offering, I'm not interested."

Moving menacingly closer, he said, "You don't mean that. What really bothers you is that you want me just as much as I want you."

"No." She took another step and felt the surf licking at her feet. Her pulse was throbbing in her temples. She had to deny what he was saying. She didn't want him. She didn't. Last night, he had been a mystery man who had appealed to her sense of romance. Today she was only dazzled by his title. If she managed to put some distance between them, she'd come to her senses.

"You think you can have any woman you want, just by asking. I'll bet the mere mention of your name would get most women into your bed."

Hot anger caused him to bait her further. "Oh, you'd be surprised how many doors my name opens. There are a lot of women who would like to sleep with royalty."

"I'm not about to become another face in the tabloids. You should stick to daughters of dukes and lords, or whatever they call themselves." Feeling herself close to tears, she turned away. "This schoolteacher from Ohio is strictly off limits."

Feeling spent and shaken, Kirsten waded through the shallows to the sailboat. Angrily Stefan snatched up the blanket and stuffed food into the hamper. Pouring the last of the champagne onto the sand, he splashed through the water close behind her.

Without a ladder, Kirsten found she couldn't climb over the side. No matter how she pulled and struggled, she kept slipping back down into the water.

For long moments, Stefan watched. Her shorts were thoroughly soaked, emphasizing an enticingly rounded bottom. Her cotton blouse clung to the curves of her body, as revealing as if she wore nothing. She was as angry as a spitting cat.

"Well, are you just going to stand there?"

A grin tugged at the corners of his mouth. "Why not? The view is terrific."

Gritting her teeth, she reached for the edge of the boat, and once more lost her grip. This time she fell beneath the waves. Coming up, she wiped the hair from her eyes and said angrily, "I need a hand into the boat."

Tossing the hamper and blanket over the rail, he waded to her side. "Put your foot in my hands. I'll lift you."

Dropping a hand to his neck, she stepped into his cupped hands. He lifted her easily, but holding on to her was a problem. She was wet and slippery. As she tumbled once more into the water, he couldn't control his laughter.

This time her anger boiled over. "You think it's funny do you?"

Catching his legs, she flipped him, sending him backward into the water. Surprised, he grabbed her and dragged her down with him. Together, they came up sputtering.

"I don't believe you did that, Stefan." She brought her palm flat against the water, sending a spray into his eyes.

"You started it." He pressed her head under the surface.

She swallowed water and came up swearing. "When I get my hands on you—"

"You'll what?" he asked, pulling her close.

The weight of the water plastered her shirt against her like a second skin, clearly outlining the soft curves of her body. When she resisted him, he pulled her roughly against him. With his hands on her shoulders, he stared down into eyes as dark as a wind-tossed sea. Deep blue, ringed with flecks of gold, they flashed storm warnings. His gaze lowered to her mouth, which was rounded in an angry pout. Without thinking, he covered her mouth with his.

She tasted of cool, salty seawater. Her skin, cold from her drenching, grew warm at his touch.

Without even knowing it, she circled his neck with her arms. Her fingers played with the wet hair at his nape. Hot flames of desire licked through her veins, warming her.

Stefan held her hips while his mouth plundered hers. Kirsten found herself responding with a helplessness that was completely out of character.

Bringing his hands up her sides, he traced the soft swell of her breasts with his thumbs, then teased her already hard nipples. With a little moan, she drew him closer. Still his thumbs continued stroking until she thought she would go mad from the touch.

"Kirsten." He breathed her name, clinging to her as the waves pushed and nudged them.

A giant wave engulfed them, nearly knocking them off their feet. Steadying himself and holding her firmly against him, Stefan stared down into her eyes. They were heavy lidded; her lips were parted for his kiss.

"Come on," he muttered, steering her toward the bobbing sailboat. "If I don't take you home right this minute, I'm going to end up taking you back to that beach. And this time I won't care how much of an audience we draw."

As they hoisted the sails and started back, Kirsten caught sight of the boat off to their left. His ever-present bodyguards. As she lifted her face to the wind, she saw the glint of sunlight off glass. Another boat? Focusing Stefan's binoculars, she scanned the horizon. There. Far to their stern. A sleek, silver-hulled speedboat. Adjusting the powerful binoculars, she strove to see more. All she could make out was someone studying her through similar lenses.

More of Stefan's men? She turned, about to ask him. Studying his proud profile, she decided against it. She'd already made too much of his lack of privacy. Besides, who but his own men would dare to come this close and spy on the prince of Maurab? His armed guards would never permit strangers so near.

Choosing silence, she turned away, dismissing the prickly feeling that nagged at the back of her mind. She was uncomfortably aware of the eyes watching her across the water. Rubbing the gooseflesh on her arms, she blamed it on the chill wind.

When Stefan dropped his arm around her shoulders, she moved closer, absorbing his warmth as well as his strength.

Chapter Four

King Alaric watched his eldest son drain a glass of wine and put down his knife and fork. Sipping black coffee, the king lifted a cigarette from a jewel-encrusted case. Instantly a white-gloved waiter snapped the flame of a lighter and bent forward. Drawing deeply, the king stared across the table through a haze of aromatic smoke.

"You didn't care for the dinner?"

Stefan shrugged. "I'm not very hungry." He toyed with a spoon.

"Late lunch?" Again the king's stare was probing. His son's handsome, rugged face gave away nothing. "Have you been feeling well lately?"

"I'm fine."

"Fine enough to go sailing all day," his youngest brother, Michael, interjected.

"Really?" The king's interest was sparked. "You should have mentioned it. I had the afternoon free."

"I took a friend."

Beside Stefan, Michael grinned and helped himself to rich chocolate mousse.

The king chose not to pursue the subject. Instead, he turned his attention to his daughter. "It's good to have you home, Alana, even if it is only for a little while. I miss you while you're in school. How did the opening of the new hospital wing go this afternoon?"

"Without a hitch. Dr. Devane is thrilled about the new CAT scan. He says we're going to have one of the best-equipped hospitals in the Mediterranean."

Alana's dark hair shimmered in the candlelight. Her laughing brown eyes seemed lit by some inner fire. The king felt the momentary jolt he experienced so often when his daughter became the mirror image of her dead mother.

Smiling, she turned to her oldest brother. "You should have come, Stefan. The staff was so excited. They wanted to share this day with all of us."

"I'll be there next week. I promised to visit the pediatrics ward."

"And you, Andrew." The king turned to his middle son. "Why weren't you at the hospital opening today?"

"Couldn't fit it in. Flying today. Remember?"

The king's eyes narrowed at his son's tousled hair and carelessly knotted tie. Appearances had never mattered to Andrew. He was happiest in a tattered fisherman's sweater and baggy pants.

"Flying. Sailing. Do none of my sons have time for official business anymore?"

"It was business. I was fulfilling my air force requirements. If I didn't take care of it today, I would've had to let it go until I returned with the U.N. delegation next month."

The king had allowed himself to forget for a moment that one of his sons was leaving the country. Each time his children left, he realized how vulnerable they were, how helpless against outside forces. He preferred to keep his family around him to stave off the loneliness that sometimes threatened to swamp him. He'd lost so many of the ones he loved: Catherine, his beloved queen; their firstborn son, Alexander, and his bride, Ann Marie. All dead. His family was shrinking. His loved ones were leaving. And each time, a part of him died.

"Who can I beat tonight at chess?" The king's smile encompassed all the members of his family. His gaze lingered on his eldest. "Stefan. It's time I trounced you."

"Not tonight, Father. I'm going out."

"Walking the beach again with Bruno?"

His son shrugged and reached for a cigarette.

Alaric's smile faded. Stefan had been agitated throughout the evening. Before dinner he'd prowled the library like a caged lion. Even though the chef had prepared a perfect chateaubriand, one of Stefan's favorite meals, he'd barely tasted it. When a waiter bent to light Stefan's third cigarette of the evening, his father's eyes narrowed. "You've learned to smoke too much."

"I had a good teacher."

It's getting to him, Alaric thought morosely. Whenever his moody, restless son stayed too long in one place, he became troubled. It had been this way since he was a boy. To Stefan, boarding schools were prisons. Summers spent exploring the Greek Isles or the ancient Oriental ruins were heaven. But summers confined to his own small country were sources of endless conflict between father and son.

When Alexander, the heir apparent, was alive, it hadn't mattered so much. The thought of his first-born caused Alaric a twinge of pain that was unexpectedly sharp. Alex had always accepted his role as future king with grace and dignity. If he'd found his strictly regimented life-style too confining, he'd never let it show. The European princess he had chosen for his bride was the perfectly trained mate. Together they had systematically assumed the tedious travel, the public appearances required of a royal couple.

Since their death, the royal duties had fallen to Stefan. It was obvious that he considered them a burden. The older man let out a sigh.

Stefan pushed his chair away from the table and walked to his father's side. Placing a hand on his shoulder, he said softly, "Good night, Father. We'll talk. Soon."

As he strode from the room, Andrew watched his brother in thoughtful silence. Glancing at his father, he muttered, "I think Stefan is contemplating one of his cruises. You'd better prepare yourself, Father. If he doesn't find a way to relieve the pressure, the top of his head's going to blow off." Andrew chuckled.

"How about the Caribbean? Maybe a few weeks of diving for treasure will cure his restlessness."

Alana shot her brother a silencing look. "Didn't you say you had to fly to Morocco, Father? Why not let Stefan take your place. I've heard that two of the sultan's best Arabians are going up for sale. Stefan's never been able to resist prizewinning horseflesh."

King Alaric's head turned so he could study his daughter. "You have a point." He seemed to consider for a moment. "I'm worried about Stefan, too. It's obvious that he's growing restless. If only I could find some way to hold his interest here."

Licking the last of the chocolate mousse from his spoon, Michael mused, "You're all off base."

The king turned to his youngest son with a smile of indulgence. "I'm afraid we all know Stefan too well to be fooled by his behavior. He never could stand to be closed in."

"If you ask me," Michael muttered, pausing to drain a full glass of milk, "he's been acting more like a man in love than a man confined."

The king's jaw dropped slightly. He went very still. Turning his head, he studied Michael. With a look of astonishment, he said, "What do you know that the rest of us have missed?"

"Stefan met a beautiful tourist on the beach. This morning they had breakfast at the villa. She went sailing with him. He was seen kissing her in a secluded cove. And if anyone would like to cover my bet, I'll lay ten he's seeing her again tonight."

"How do you manage to know all this?"

Michael saw the gleam of interest in his father's eyes. "I have my sources."

"Have you been gambling with the palace staff again?"

At Michael's mock-innocent look, the king added, "No matter. A woman." Alaric stubbed out his cigarette. "Ten dollars, you say?" At his son's nod, he chuckled. "This is one bet I hope I lose."

His children watched as Alaric's stern dark eyes crinkled with good humor. He tapped a finger eagerly on the table. "A woman. Of course. What better way to keep him happy in Maurab then to settle him down with a wife and children? He's thirty-one now. It's time he found the love of a good woman."

"Father." Alana's voice broke through his racing thoughts. "If Michael's right—" she shot her youngest brother a cutting look "—and I'm not at all sure about the reliability of his sources, all it means is that Stefan has met a beautiful tourist. That's a far cry from love and marriage."

The king was fairly beaming now. Nothing could staunch the flow of his plans. "You saw him. He was as tense as a panther." He stood and clapped his youngest son on the back. "Nothing can put a man more on edge than a woman. Nothing. And nothing can settle a man down faster than the love of a good woman. Come on, Michael. I haven't beaten you at chess in a week or more."

"More like a month. The last three times we played, I won. But I don't mind giving you one more lesson."

With a roar of laughter, Alaric dropped an arm around the shoulders of his son and led the way to the wood-paneled game room.

In the west wing of the palace, Stefan entered his private apartment and strode to the bedroom. The dog lying in the corner of the room raised his head. At the sight of his master, the dog thumped his tail on the floor rhythmically. Bounding forward, he pushed his face into Stefan's waiting hand.

"You know what time it is, don't you, Bruno?"

The dog panted in answer.

"You'll get your walk. You need it. We both do. We're two of a kind, you and I. Restless souls."

Stripping off his suit jacket and tie, Stefan unbuttoned his shirt and dropped it on the bed. His father always insisted on formal attire for their family meals.

The clothes he'd requested earlier had been carefully laid out by his valet. Picking up a cashmere sweater, he paused, seeing the shimmer of the crimson sunset reflected on the rough waves far below. He leaned a hip against the marble sill and studied the flight of a seabird as it dipped and soared, then joined its mate high above the rocky cliffs.

The cool evening breeze whispered across his naked chest, and he thought of gentle hands caressing him. All evening he'd thought of nothing except Kirsten. Kirsten. Just the sound of her name stirred his restless heart. He had never believed in love at first sight. He'd never understood old friends who were so bewitched by a woman that they became fools for love. Yet from the moment he'd seen her standing on that darkened beach looking too lovely to belong to this world, he'd felt a quickening of his heart, a heating of his blood.

Turning away from the window, he pulled the sweater over his head and yanked roughly on the sleeves. There was a simple explanation for his reaction. He's been confined in his little country for too long now. He needed the stimulation of travel. An exotic trip, a few beautiful women, and he would come to his senses. He'd been dubbed the playboy prince by the world's press since he was twenty-one. And he'd earned the reputation. He was certainly too old and worldly-wise to be snared by a pretty face.

He picked up the leash, then discarded it. Neither he nor Bruno cared for leashes or tethers of any kind. He headed for the private stairs that led to an enclosed courtyard. The dog bounded ahead of him and stood whining at the door.

They passed through the formal gardens and paved walkways. Far ahead of him, the dog paused at the locked gate and waited impatiently until a uniformed guard unlocked it and swung it wide.

Following a rocky path along the cliffs, they wound their way on a treacherous downward course, until they encountered the white sandy beach that encircled the outer perimeter of the land like a jeweled necklace.

Freedom. The dog raced ahead, chasing the surf, then turning to dodge it as it rolled over his paws.

As always, Stefan found himself breathing deeply of the brisk, salty breeze. Why did the air smell sweeter beyond the gates of the palace? Like Bruno, he felt the need to escape the walls, to chase the waves, to break free.

He picked up a stone and tossed it into the surf, chuckling when the dog jumped into the water and returned with the prize in his mouth. Dropping it at his master's feet, Bruno poised himself for the next chase. Far along the beach, man and dog played the game, each anticipating the other's moves.

Though he tried to appear at ease, Stefan felt his muscles tighten as he drew nearer the villa. She would be there, on the beach. Earlier today, he'd explained that his father demanded that the entire family gather for a private dinner twice a week. Since his early childhood, the routine had never varied. Those family members in residence were expected to gather for a review of their public appearances as representatives of the country. Stefan had often found these family meals tedious. Tonight, thinking of the lovely woman who'd captured his thoughts, he'd found it especially difficult to be patient. But then he wasn't a patient man. He was accustomed to having what he wanted, when he wanted it. And what he wanted was Kirsten.

She stood on the moon-drenched beach absorbed in the beauty of her exotic surroundings. The sunset had been a spectacular display. The heavens had turned to fire. Clouds, shot with gold, drifted on the horizon. The sea slowly swallowed up the sun, turning the waves to flame. Despite the rising full moon, the velvet sky twinkled with millions of tiny lights.

Settling herself on a rock, Kirsten drew a shawl around her shoulders and fought down the urge to run back to her villa. Stefan wouldn't come. Ever since he had deposited her at the door of her cottage, she'd been fighting this battle with herself. His story that he was compelled to dine with his family tonight was plausible enough. But the longer they were apart, the more convinced she was that she'd been a fool. He was a prince. His entire life had been one of indulgence and glamour. There couldn't possibly be a place in his world for a schoolteacher from a small town in the United States. He had taken her sailing on a whim. Now that he'd satisfied his curiosity about her, she would never see him again. What could they possibly have in common?

Kirsten tried to recall everything they had discussed today. There was so much. They had laughed and talked endlessly. He'd been fascinating and charming and even funny. But for the life of her, she couldn't recall a single thing she'd said. What a bore her life must seem by comparison. How could he possibly find her interesting?

Slipping off her shoes, she felt the sand, still warm from the sun. The breeze ruffled her hair, and she absently tucked it behind her ear. Why was she tormenting herself like this? She'd never see the prince again. Still, it would make an interesting memory for her later years. Of course, nobody in Fairfield would believe her. With a little sigh of impatience, she stood and brushed off the skirt of the delicately embroidered sundress she'd worn to dinner at the hotel. Turning from the shore, she saw the shadowy outline of a man and dog. Both were standing very still. Both were watching her.

His nerves were strung to their limit. The relief he felt at the sight of her left him weak. "I knew you'd be here," he murmured, moving a step closer.

She glanced at the ridge of the hill and saw the silhouette of his two guards. Her smile of happiness faded slightly. In a haughty tone she replied, "I'll have to remember not to be so predictable. How was dinner with your family?"

She heard the warmth of his laughter. "Predictable." He took another step so that they were nearly touching. Reaching up, he caught an errant strand of her hair and twisted it around his finger. He felt the familiar quickening the moment he touched her.

"And all the while I kept wishing I was having dinner in some exotic place with you."

She looked up into eyes that glinted in the moonlight. His warm breath feathered the hair at her temple and warmed her skin.

"Where would we go, if you could choose any place on earth?"

He thought a moment. "There's a little temple in Tibet, nestled between two towering mountain peaks. It takes three days with Sherpa guides to reach it. The sun glistens on snow so dazzling it almost blinds you. The land is frozen, and silent, and completely untouched. Inside the temple, there's the smell of incense and spices. Except for chanting at dawn and dusk, there is only silence."

Stefan's hands dropped to her shoulders. His fingers toyed with the tiny bands of lace that secured her dress. "The monks create exotic meals, combinations of bland and spicy foods, topped off with little pastries that melt in your mouth, and the strongest, richest coffee you've ever tasted."

Kirsten inhaled his musky scent and fought the desire to touch him. His dog, though quiet, stood stiffly beside him. She knew, without looking, that the men on the hilltop were watching intently.

"It's so quiet there, you can hear your own heart beat. I've felt a peace, a contentment there, that I've never found anywhere else on earth. You'd swear when you left that you'd just been to heaven."

"Why did you visit the temple?"

He smiled and she felt an odd little thrill. "Because it was there."

"Is there any place you haven't visited?"

"A few," he said matter-of-factly. "But I intend to see them all before I die."

"Why?"

He ran his thumbs along her arms, feeling the satin softness of her skin. He wanted to crush her to him and feel the familiar rush of passion he knew she could unleash. Instead, he contented himself with the sound of her husky voice and the soft summer scent of her.

"There's a restlessness in me, Kirsten. I can't explain it. I only know that I'm constantly driven to see new places, try new things."

He felt her stiffen slightly. "And I suppose it's novel for you to spend time with me. Is that why you've singled me out? Because I'm different from the other women you know?"

His hands gripped her upper arms roughly. She could feel the pressure of his thumbs against her tender skin. His voice hardened. "Oh, I don't know you,

Kirsten. At least not yet. But I intend to." His face lowered until his lips were almost touching hers. His breath was hot. His tone was low and angry. "I intend to know everything about you. What you like and dislike, what you think, how you feel lying in my arms."

"You're being presumptuous."

"Am I? Are you saying you have no curiosity about me?"

"None."

"Liar." His mouth covered hers in a savage kiss. Energy, raw and intense, seemed to consume them.

He hadn't intended to attack her. All evening he'd thought of nothing but Kirsten, her scent, her rich, husky voice, her taste. He'd wanted to be gentle, persuasive. He'd planned soft words, a sweet seduction. What was it about this beautiful, ethereal creature that turned him into someone he didn't even recognize?

For a moment Kirsten stiffened in his arms, shocked by the intensity of his kiss. Gradually she became aware of her hands clawing at the front of his sweater as if to hold him to her. Her blood ran hot, and she let the shawl slip unheeded from her arms and fall to the sand at their feet.

She was no longer an unwilling party to the kiss; her mouth grew hungry on his.

Stunned, Stefan caught her roughly by the shoulders and held her a little away from him. For long moments he stared down into her smoldering eyes, and then his gaze moved to her moist lips.

Slowly, slowly, until she thought her heart would burst from waiting, he lowered his head. This time his lips were gentle on hers. The hands that held her were as tender as if she were a fragile crystal sculpture. He drew her into the circle of his embrace, and his fingertips caressed the naked skin of her back, sending splinters of fire and ice along her spine.

She felt her bones melting at the tenderness of his kiss. Her arms encircled his waist, drawing him even tighter to her. She slipped her hands beneath his sweater to roam the taut flesh of his back. His body was lean and hard, an athlete's body.

Stefan explored her mouth leisurely, drinking in the sweetness. His tongue played with hers, and he felt her quick little gasp of pleasure before she gave herself up to explorations of her own. He thrust his hands into the tangle of her hair, loving the feel of it against his palms. Her delicate floral scent surrounded him until he was drowning in her. She was filling his mind, stealing his will. All he could think of was lying with her here in the warm, moon-washed sand.

Kirsten reveled in the masculine scents and tastes that were so alien to her. She identified the faint tang of brandy and the sharp bite of Turkish tobacco on his tongue. The hands that held her close and kneaded the soft flesh of her back were strong and sure. He made her feel warm and safe and protected. Too warm, too safe. She'd never needed anyone else to take care of her. Gram had taught her to look out for herself.

While her body responded to his every touch, her mind rebelled against this weakness. She was losing herself to him. It had taken her years to find herself, her strengths. If she gave in to the desire that throbbed within her, she'd lose everything she'd worked so hard to attain. Bits and pieces of herself would be surrendered to him. And with them, her strength, her will to make it alone. Hadn't she learned early in life that the only constant was herself? Everyone else she'd ever depended on was gone. And now she was risking losing everything to this man's whims.

He heard her little moan and took the kiss deeper. His need for this woman was almost overpowering.

"Stefan." Calling on her last ounce of strength, she pushed against his chest.

Lifting his head, he traced the outline of her swollen lips with his finger. She moved away from his touch, fighting the desire to lift her face for one last drugging kiss.

"I have to go back now."

"I'll walk with you."

"No." She couldn't risk having him kiss her at the door of her villa. The thought of the privacy behind that door was too tempting. "I need to be alone."

She could feel his amber gaze holding her, demanding an explanation. She had none to give.

His hands dropped to his sides. Instantly the dog stood and thrust his face into Stefan's palm. Mechanically he smoothed the rough fur.

She looked beyond him to the men on the hill. "I'd better get back. It's late."

"I'll see you in the morning."

"I've arranged for a bus tour of the city."

"Cancel it. I'll take you."

"I'm not . . ."

His hand snaked out, catching her firmly by the arm. "Dammit. It's my city. I want to show it to you."

She met his glittering, angry look. Moistening her lips with the tip of her tongue, she nodded slightly. "All right."

He relaxed. A hint of a smile lifted the corners of his lips. "Don't bother ordering breakfast. I have something special in mind."

As she turned away, he added softly, "Of course I had something special in mind tonight, too. But I suppose I have to learn I can't have everything I want."

Turning back to him, she whispered, "A very bright pupil. I like that."

He brought a hand to the back of her head and drew her face closer. "Don't expect too much from me, teacher."

Before she could pull away, he brushed her lips with his and felt her sway against him.

A moment later she stepped back and turned away. As she hurried toward her villa, she kept her back stiff, her head lifted in an arrogant pose. It wasn't until she reached her door that she gave in to the trembling that threatened to reveal just how much his touch affected her.

Chapter Five

Were the mornings always so sunny in Maurab, Kirsten wondered. Was the sky always this perfect cloudless blue? Barefoot, she perched on the brick ledge that enclosed her patio and sipped steaming coffee. Sunlight played over her hair, turning the ends to flame. She wore it long and loose, streaming down her back in a cascade of artless curls. Her only make-up was a touch of gloss on her lips. A pale peach cotton skirt with deep pockets, topped by a matching sleeveless eyelet blouse, enhanced her sun-kissed looks.

There was a storybook quality to this place, she thought, staring out to sea. Colorful sailboats dotted the calm waters. On the horizon a cruise ship drifted, emitting powder puffs of smoke. She turned her head inland. Villas with orange-tiled roofs clung to the sides of hills. Steps had been cut into the sheer rock walls that led down to the water's edge.

This was a country made for frolicking in the sun, for dreaming, for...falling in love. The mere thought left her stunned.

Kirsten paced to the patio door, a bemused smile lighting her features. She was letting this place weave its spell. Amy's fairy tales were spilling over into reality. All her life, she'd had to make hard choices, face difficult decisions. Now, finally given the opportunity to reflect, to daydream, she was allowing herself to go too far. Falling in love, she thought scornfully. Song writers made it sound as simple as falling off a log. In reality, it was more like falling off a cliff. The tumble might be breathtaking, but the landing could be shattering.

She shook her head to dispel the last lingering shadow of fantasy. Stefan was handsome, charming and an altogether wonderful companion. He was also heir to the throne of Maurab. Definitely out of her league.

Without her knowledge, the object of her disturbing thoughts stood in the shade of a flowering tree and studied the slender figure on the patio. All night she had crept, unbidden, into his dreams to taunt him. He'd awakened with a hunger sharper than any he'd ever experienced. Seeing her only further whetted his appetite. She was almost too good to be true. This day was sweeter, because it would be spent with her. He was greedy to have all her time.

He stepped closer. At the sound, she looked up.

"Why do you insist on coming in the back way? There is a front door to this villa."

"But this is so much more private."

For a moment her heart froze. "We wouldn't want anyone to know the prince was seeing the visiting schoolteacher, would we?"

"After today, the whole town will know. You'd better be prepared to become the object of local gossip. I intend to show you as much of my country as possible until it's too dark to see anything more. And while you're seeing it, you'll be seen, as well." At his quick disarming smile, her fears fled. He was showing off his country for her. And he was willing to show her off, too.

"I brought you something." He continued to hold one hand behind his back.

"Another present? Show me."

He brought his hand forward and held up a shiny apple. "For my favorite teacher. I polished it myself. Have a bite."

With a grin, she bit into the apple. "Umm. Delicious."

Watching her, Stefan couldn't resist bringing his lips to hers. She tasted of tart apple.

"Here," she said, "if you're that hungry, you finish it."

"It isn't apple I want." For long moments he stared down at her surprised look. "Come on." He caught her hand. "I can see I'm wasting my time." With a quick glance at her feet he added dryly, "You'll need shoes."

"Darn. I thought I could travel in comfort and leave my shoes behind today." With a sudden laugh, she bounded away and returned carrying a pair of sandals. "We wouldn't want to scandalize the good people of Maurab, would we?"

Holding hands like blissful young lovers, they strolled to his waiting car.

The sleek black Ferrari turned off the narrow road. Gravel crunched under the wheels. As the car came to a halt before the chalet, intricately carved wooden doors were thrown open and a white-haired man hurried along a flagstone walk.

While Stefan assisted Kirsten from the car, the man beamed his welcome.

"Good morning, Hugo."

"Prince Stefan. Everything is ready. How kind of you to grace our little inn with your presence."

"This is Kirsten Stevens."

Kirsten found herself staring into sparkling blue eyes. The old man's face was wreathed in a smile, adding to the network of fine lines that etched his face.

"Welcome to Hugo's, Miss Stevens."

"Thank you."

As they followed their host, Stefan kept his hand lightly beneath her arm. Even that small contact sent shock waves rippling through her. When was she going to stop reacting this way to his every touch? She hoped her face didn't look as heated as her blood.

Inside the small inn, they were led across gleaming stone floors to a sunny window which overlooked a formal English garden. Stefan sat beside her on a settee covered in colorful floral chintz. An antique table of cherry wood was set for two with fine bone china and delicate crystal. All about the room Kirsten could see evidence of the love and care that had gone into this elegant old inn.

Logs were stacked carefully in the fireplace. On the hearth rested a porcelain cat. On the mantel, silver candlesticks stood guard beside an ornate silver tray.

The garden showed the same care that had been given everything else in this place. Hedges were meticulously trimmed. Borders of colorful flowers had been planted with an eye to size and texture. Silver leaves showed off deep purple blooms. Brilliant reds were surrounded by delicate white buds. A brick wall was covered with thousands of pink climbing roses. Their perfume drifted in the open window, mingling with the wonderful aroma of freshly baked pastries.

"Hugo's Inn has been an institution in my country since my father was a boy. Hugo and his wife, Marta, oversee everything about the operation."

"It's lovely, Stefan."

"I wanted you to start your day here." He lifted her hand and traced the long, slender fingers. "Creative. The hands of an artist."

She shook her head, trying to deny her feelings as much as his words. "You forget. Just a Sunday painter. I'm afraid I don't have the talent to be anything more." She chuckled, and the sound made him smile. "I do some mean caricatures, though. Every year I reward my students by drawing a caricature of each of them. Of course I enhance their good points instead of their bad."

"I want you to do one of me."

He saw the quick flash of humor in her eyes. "I warn you. In your case, I won't be kind."

"Good. I prefer honesty." He smiled at the young waitress who was pouring their coffee. "Carla, would you bring us a pencil and paper, please?"

The girl nodded and hurried away. A moment later she returned with a pad of paper and several pencils.

While Stefan watched, Kirsten made quick, strong strokes on the page. With only an occasional glance at him, she drew from memory, adding shadowed, mysterious eyes and gleaming white teeth. At his side she sketched his dog, with oversize head and bared fangs. With a flourish, she handed the paper over for his inspection.

The drawing showed razor-short hair, a wide forehead furrowed in concentration, and eyes ringed with long, thick lashes. Despite the emphasis on hooded eyes and a wicked smile, the resemblance was uncanny. She'd added bulging muscles to his arms, and boating shoes on small stick feet. Above his head hovered a crown.

He threw back his head and roared. "It's perfect."

"Maybe you could have it framed and hang it with the royal portraits. You do have royal portraits, don't you?"

"We do. But this one is for my eyes only. I have no intention of sharing it with the world."

She watched as he rolled it carefully and placed it in his shirt pocket.

Their waitress returned with steaming platters of smoked sausage and coddled eggs, along with delicate glazed pastries filled with cinnamon and nuts.

"Oh, Stefan, this is the only way to start the day." As she ate, Kirsten added, "I'm going to remember this when I'm running out the door with a lukewarm cup of coffee."

"Why must you always run?"

"Because I tend to oversleep. And I oversleep," she added, anticipating his next question, "because I stay up too late at night grading papers and planning my next class assignments. I'm always striving for order and discipline. It's the only way I know how to function."

He watched as she bit into a delicate pastry. Rolling her eyes heavenward, she murmured, "Oh, this is wonderful."

He grinned at her simple pleasure and brushed a crumb from the corner of her lips. "I detest order and discipline. It goes against the grain." His voice lowered. "Man wasn't meant to awaken to the sound of a bell, and to sleep simply because the lights have been turned out."

She turned to study his features, which had suddenly become stern. "Do I detect a complaint here. You sound like a recording of a new army recruit."

"Navy." His smile slowly returned. "It's a necessary part of our education. Every male member of the Maurab royal family must train in one of the country's armed services."

"And you chose the navy."

He nodded. "I spent years in military schools and hated them. But I've always loved sailing. On the water I feel free."

"But you resented the routine."

"Only the hours. I love the sea. And I could handle any assignment. But I hated the sound of bells."

"Mutinous talk." She chuckled. "Any sailor worth his salt should know how to rise at dawn."

"If I'd had someone like you to look at, I might have handled it better." Brushing a strand of hair from her cheek, he stared at her until she felt herself blushing under his scrutiny.

"Come on," he said suddenly. "Before we leave, we have to speak with Hugo and Marta."

The elderly owners were in the kitchen, instructing their staff. All about them, counter tops and copper pots gleamed. It was obvious they lavished as much attention on their private quarters as they did on the public rooms of the inn.

"Marta, I'd like you to meet Kirsten Stevens."

The old woman turned from the stove. Smiling, she extended her hand, peering closely at the younger woman.

"I hope everything was done to your satisfaction," she said.

"It was perfect. Thank you."

"You are American?"

Kirsten nodded.

In a heavily accented voice, Marta asked, "How long will you be in Maurab?"

"Not nearly long enough," Kirsten said with a laugh. "I have less than two weeks to see everything."

The old woman saw the tiny frown that marred the prince's forehead. "Perhaps you can be persuaded to extend your stay." Marta looked beyond her to the young man whose gaze never left Kirsten's face. "Come." She placed an arm around Kirsten's shoulders. "Let me show you our gardens before you leave."

"I was admiring them from the window. Tell me, how long have you and Hugo been here?"

"I came here from Eastern Europe as a young girl. My parents and I escaped when our country was overrun by troops. I had thought about America. But when I met Hugo here, I realized I had already found my destiny."

As the two women moved outside, their voices faded.

Hugo turned to the prince. "Did you tell your young lady that Marta likes nothing better than to talk about her childhood?"

Stefan shook his head and continued to watch as the two women toured the formal gardens. Their voices were a low hum. "Kirsten seems to have a natural instinct about people. And a seeking, curious mind."

"She has won Marta's heart forever by showing an interest in the gardens. Your young woman is as kind as she is beautiful."

The prince, Hugo noted, continued to study the slender figure through the window. As the two returned, their voices gradually rose above the kitchen sounds.

"You can't possibly see everything in Maurab in two weeks. Why not extend your visit?"

"I'm afraid I can't. I have to get back to my classroom."

"Ah. You teach." The older woman's features softened. "The world will never have enough good teachers. We could use her talents here, Prince Stefan."

He tore his gaze away from Kirsten's face long enough to smile at his hostess. "Indeed we could. Thank you, Marta." He turned to include her husband. "Hugo. I promised Kirsten a perfect beginning to our day together. Breakfast was as special as I'd hoped."

As they turned to leave, Marta said, "You will bring your young lady back, I trust? We would be honored."

The prince turned and winked. "I'll see if it can be arranged."

As they drove away, the prince marveled at the ease with which his companion managed to win the hearts of everyone she came in contact with.

"This casino is one of the oldest in Europe. For many years it was the great attraction of our country for the moneyed and titled tourists." All day Stefan had played the part of tour guide. While the facts rolled off his tongue, he savored the company of the fascinating woman beside him. "But I suspect our yacht harbors and excellent restaurants are equally attractive now.''

Only a man who truly loved his country could find so many fascinating things to say about it. ''Do you have many permanent residents?'' Kirsten asked.

Stefan turned to her, loving the way her eyes sparkled with intelligence and humor. All day, her interest in his country had never waned.

''Like your country, we attract a great many immigrants. Citizens of Maurab pay no taxes.'' He laughed at the way her eyes widened at this piece of information. ''They enjoy the benefits of free education and medical care. And we are ideally located for international travel.'' His voice warmed with emotion. ''To see my country is to love it. After only one visit, it's difficult to leave. At least,'' he added with an arched brow, ''I hope in your case that will be true.''

She turned to him, momentarily blinded by the reflection of sunlight off dazzling marble walls. It wasn't, she told herself firmly, the sight of the handsome man who blinded her. ''Stefan, I have no choice. When my two weeks are up, I must leave.''

Shaking off a vague feeling of discontent, he took her arm as they crossed to a fountain in the center of the square. ''We won't speak of it again. We'll speak only of pleasant things.''

She couldn't hide the smile that touched her lips at his words. He wasn't about to allow anything to mar this day.

''Here,'' he said, pointing, ''is the new university. My father realized how difficult it was for parents to send their children far from home to further their education. So he insisted on the construction of a college here in the heart of the city. He staffed it with the finest educators from all over the world. In that way, he introduced languages and customs that have broadened the horizons of his citizens."

Kirsten heard the note of pride in Stefan's voice. "Your father takes his job seriously, doesn't he?"

"Being king isn't an honorary title. It requires care and thought, and hard work. He works harder than anyone will ever realize." Stunned by the vehemence of his words, he paused, then slowly smiled. "Don't let him know I said that. We argue constantly about the place of royalty in society. I wouldn't have him think I agreed with him."

Kirsten chuckled as he held the door of his car for her. Settling inside, she said, "Don't worry. Your secret is safe with me."

In the gathering dusk the streetlights came on, bathing the city in a hazy green glow. Stefan drove slowly, allowing Kirsten to enjoy the tranquility of his city.

"Oh, look." She pointed to a full moon rising just above the tops of the buildings.

"I ordered it just for you."

"Amazing. What else can you do?"

"Anything. Just ask."

Kirsten turned to him with a smile. "I wish you could stop time, so we could hold on to this day."

"Now you ask too much." He followed the curving ribbon of drive along the water's edge and stopped in front of her villa. "But we can make the day last a little longer. Have dinner with me."

"I don't think so."

He turned off the ignition. Evening sounds broke the silence. Insects whirred. A lone gull cried. Somewhere in the distance, the music of an orchestra rose and fell.

"Why?" In the darkness he reached a finger to her cheek and felt her stiffen at his touch.

"It's been a long day."

"Not nearly long enough. I know a secluded place."

"No." Her heart lodged in her throat. Each time he touched her, her reaction was the same. She couldn't risk being alone with him.

"A very public place, then." His voice was warm with laughter.

"Stefan, I'm too tired." Lying to him was easier than dealing with her emotions.

"Come on." He caught her hand and helped her from the car. When they reached the door of her villa, he took her key and pushed the door open. "I'll be back in an hour," he said firmly. "Be ready."

"Didn't you listen? I said I was too tired."

Catching her by the shoulders, he pulled her close and stared down into her startled eyes. His voice was dangerously soft. "You're no more tired than I. Stop fighting it, Kirsten. Our being together is inevitable."

She swallowed, and his knowing smile sent tremors along her spine.

"An hour," he repeated, brushing his lips across hers. "And even that will seem like an eternity."

*　*　*

Stefan took the steps three at a time. One hour. In an hour, he'd be with Kirsten again. His heart was lighter than he could ever remember it being. Pushing open the door to his private apartment, he stripped his shirt off over his head on the way to the shower. Halfway across the room, he paused.

A figure was seated in the chair in the corner.

"You've been gone all day, Stefan," his father said.

"Yes." He stiffened. "Is something wrong?"

The king's eyes were hidden in shadow. His voice sounded not so much stern as eager. "Nothing. Are you going out again?"

"In an hour. I was heading for the shower." He rubbed his shoulders to ease the tension that had crept into them. "I assume there's a reason for this visit."

The king's fingers tapped a rhythm on the arm of the chair. "I have it on good authority that you're seeing a young woman. An American."

"And?" The shirt dangled, forgotten, in Stefan's hand.

"Did you spend the day with her?"

"Yes."

"And last night, after dinner, did you see her?"

"I did." His eyes narrowed.

"I want to meet her."

"Why?"

The king's voice was entirely too soothing. He had something up his sleeve. "I shouldn't have to explain myself to you, Stefan. I want to meet this American tourist. Unless, of course, there's some reason why I shouldn't."

"I hardly know her myself. I have no intention of subjecting her to an inspection by the entire family."

"Are you ashamed of her?"

"Don't be ridiculous."

"Is she another of your meaningless flirtations?"

Stefan flinched, and found, to his discomfort, that he couldn't say the words that would have ended this interrogation. Meaningless? Maybe that was what he would have called it a day ago. And now? He was no longer certain of anything, except the fact that he had to see Kirsten again.

"So." The king had watched his son closely. Now he folded his hands calmly in his lap. "The Duke and Duchess of Kentshire are here on a visit. Since Andrew is going away next week, I thought this would be a good time to have a formal dinner."

Stefan strained to see his father's face. "And you waited up here to tell me that?"

"I waited up here to see for myself what you have just told me. I want you to bring your... American tourist to the dinner."

"She isn't used to our ways. She lives a very simple life in America. I don't think she'd be comfortable at a formal dinner."

"I'll be the judge of that." He stood. "Tomorrow night. We'll have drinks in the library before dinner. Just the immediate family. She'll have a chance to meet us before the guests arrive."

As Stefan opened his mouth to argue, the king snapped, "Bring her."

The prince stormed across the room, roughly yanking open the door to the shower.

"By the way. What is the girl's name?"

Stefan turned, glowering. Through gritted teeth, he hissed, "Kirsten." His tone immediately softened. "Kirsten Stevens."

The king nodded. "I look forward to meeting your Kirsten."

Outside the door, the king paused, deep in thought. Could it be that Stefan didn't even know yet how much he cared for this woman? It was obvious that he needed only to speak her name and his tone warmed.

By God. The older man turned away, a smile creasing his handsome face. What fools these young lovers could be.

But he would know. The minute he saw them together, he'd know, even if they didn't.

He hurried down the stairs. Now where was Michael tonight? He owed his youngest son ten dollars.

Chapter Six

Kirsten set aside her hair dryer and angrily dragged a brush through the tangles. Why had she allowed Stefan to talk her into dinner tonight? The day had been so idyllic. They had walked and talked and held hands like any other couple. He had taken such pains to show her all the highlights of his country. All day Stefan had been the perfect gentleman. But just beneath that cool facade, she'd sensed a simmering passion. From the beginning, Stefan had made it clear that he wanted her. Now it was going to become necessary to put some distance between them. Because, though she tried to deny it, she was finding it more and more difficult to fight the attraction she felt for him. Tonight would surely lead to another battle of wills.

When they were apart, it was easy for her to remind herself who he was. But whenever they were together, he ceased being the prince. He was a man. A handsome, virile man who made her respond like a woman. This whole situation was impossible.

In a fit of anger she did something completely out of character. She hurled the hairbrush across the room. It fell with a muffled thud just as a knock sounded on the door.

Smoothing her narrow rose silk dress over her hips, she walked to the door, reminding herself to keep control of the evening. They would have dinner and a few laughs. Nothing more.

All her cool promises dissolved when she opened the door and stared up into Stefan's laughing, confident eyes.

"My kind of woman. Ready exactly on time. I brought you flowers."

Any other man would have brought her roses, or a lavish bouquet. But Stefan wasn't like any man she'd ever known. She stared at a nosegay of tiny, perfect violets.

"Oh, they're beautiful." She buried her face in them to hide the little tear that sprang to her eye.

"Not nearly as beautiful as the woman holding them."

"How did you know I love violets?"

She lifted glistening eyes to him. Stefan was wearing a dark suit and white shirt with a carefully knotted silk tie. The right cuff of his shirt bore his monogram. On his left wrist, a gold watch gleamed in the lamplight.

"A lucky guess. Or maybe I'm beginning to know more about you than you think." He glanced at his watch. "An hour was too long to be away. I should have come sooner." His gaze swept the mass of hair that framed her lovely face. As always, she took his breath away. The rich tone of her dress added color to her cheeks. She was the only woman he knew who needed no makeup to enhance her beauty. To him, she was perfect.

"Any earlier and you'd have caught me in the shower."

"I'm very good at scrubbing backs."

"Really? Another of your many accomplishments?"

He caught a strand of her hair and felt its silken texture between his fingers. "I'm good at other things, as well."

"I'll just bet you are." She crossed the room on the pretext of finding a vase. The truth was, she needed to evade his touch. Did he have any idea what he did to her?

Placing the violets in a little round vase, she set them on the table and paused to admire their delicate beauty.

"Ready?"

She picked up a small beaded bag and nodded. "You did say we'd go someplace with lots of people."

He'd hoped she'd forgotten. "If you insist."

In answer, she simply smiled and took his arm.

Despite the darkness outside, she noted a car idling behind his. "When do your men eat?"

He helped her into the Ferrari and walked to the other side. Turning on the ignition, he said, "They'll eat while we eat. At another table, of course." He grinned. "Unless you'd like them to join us."

She refused to take the bait. "That could be fun. I may find I like being surrounded by strong, silent men. What do you think?"

"I think, Miss Stevens, that I would like you all to myself. I know a very private apartment where we could be alone."

She shot him a frigid look. "You promised—"

He cut her off with an exasperated sigh. "And you'll never let me forget it."

She leaned back and smiled in the darkness.

The car sped along the narrow twisting streets, climbing steadily until they reached a building that seemed to cling to the side of a hill. As soon as the car came to a stop, a doorman hurried forward. Stepping out, Kirsten paused to look down on the city spread out below them. Green and gold lights shimmered like tiny jewels. Standing beside her, Stefan caught her hand.

"Whenever I return from abroad, this is the view that excites me."

She turned to him with a smile. "I think you're a little bit fond of your country."

"A little." He allowed his gaze to sweep her from head to toe. "But this sight excites me more."

As she drew away, he laughed. "Come on. You'll enjoy Marcella."

"Marcella?"

"Our hostess."

Together they climbed wide marble stairs. Though the restaurant was an immense room, the private booths separated by etched glass and hanging plants created a sense of intimacy.

The maître d' led them to their table. A few minutes later Stefan ordered wine. While the waiter was filling their stemmed glasses, a stately, elegant woman hurried toward them with her arms outstretched. Immediately Stefan rose to greet her.

"Stefan, you devil. It's been too long."

"Marcella. I've missed you. You look wonderful." He kissed both her cheeks, then turned. "I want you to meet Kirsten Stevens." His hand dropped possessively to Kirsten's shoulder. "Kirsten, this is Marcella Sainte Amour."

Kirsten found herself staring into the darkest eyes she'd ever seen. They were so dark that the pupil and iris were almost indistinguishable. By contrast, the woman's skin was pale, almost translucent. Even though she had carefully applied makeup, blue veins were visible just beneath the surface. Her hair, worn in a coronet of braids, was as black as a raven's wing. Her gown was heavy ruby velvet. At her throat gleamed a necklace of enormous rubies and diamonds. Though no longer young, she was still an exotic beauty.

"Kirsten." The woman extended her hand, then sat down. "Something about the way Stefan speaks your name makes me think you are not just another pretty face."

Taken by surprise, Kirsten soon found that she liked this woman's outspoken manner.

"Did you know that Kirsten means 'the anointed one?'"

Kirsten glanced over to see Stefan watching the old woman closely. Turning her attention back to Marcella, she responded, "I had no idea what my name means. How did you know?"

"I've made it my business to study names." She smiled easily. "Our king is well named. Alaric means 'ruler of all.'" For a moment the old woman's eyes darkened. "When Stefan was named, Alaric asked me for the meaning of the name his wife had chosen for his young son. He was certain I was wrong when I told him. And he even considered changing it. Because, of course, the king's second son was not meant to be king."

Kirsten couldn't contain her curiosity. "What does Stefan mean?"

"Crown," the old woman said firmly.

She suddenly gave a brilliant smile. "Where did you two meet?"

"On the beach. Stefan was walking his dog. And I was ... just staring at the stars."

"Making wishes?"

Kirsten laughed self-consciously. "I'm too old for wishes."

"We're never too old. Of course," the old woman added, "*being* is better than wishing." Turning Kirsten's palm up, she asked, "If you could have any wish you wanted, what would it be?"

Kirsten didn't respond. She dared not speak her heart's desire. It would be bad luck.

When Marcella glanced up, she saw the flush staining the young woman's cheeks. "You were raised in an orderly environment and taught hard work and discipline." Marcella sighed. "But it is your nature to be dreamy and creative. All your life these two sides of your personality have warred within you."

Kirsten looked down. "Practicality wins out every time."

Marcella was quick to note the little frown line on Stefan's forehead. Of all people, he would understand this inner conflict.

Quickly filling the silence, the older woman traced a finger over Kirsten's open hand. "Ah. You have a long lifeline. I see love. Here." She touched a long, painted fingernail to a line in Kirsten's palm. "And I see many children."

"I teach many children," Kirsten explained, to cover her embarrassment.

"These are not other people's children. These are yours. You will enjoy much happiness. But first I see—" Marcella's eyes narrowed. For a moment a tiny frown line appeared between her eyes. She appeared deeply distressed. Kirsten cast a worried glance at Stefan, then looked back at the old woman's face. As quickly as it had appeared, the frown vanished. She looked up with a too-bright smile. Covering the young woman's hand with her own, Marcella pressed them tightly together, as if absorbing some secret pain. She turned abruptly to Stefan, her eyes darkening. "Where are your men?"

"Across the room. There." He inclined his head slightly.

She strained to make them out in the dim light. "Good. I will see to their wishes." Marcella fixed him with a look. "You tend to be careless, my young friend. See that you look over your shoulder once in a while."

She seemed about to say more when the maître d' interrupted, bending to whisper to her, then pointing toward the door.

Immediately her manner became professional. "I must say good-night to some old patrons. Enjoy your dinner."

Standing, Stefan brushed his lips over her hand. Tenderly she touched his cheek, then gave the young couple a lingering look. With a rush of nervous energy, she was gone.

"What was that all about?"

Seeing Kirsten's troubled look, Stefan squeezed her hand. His old friend had a very special gift. Of that he had no doubt. But he couldn't alarm Kirsten. "Marcella dabbles in the occult. Don't mind her. She enjoys being dramatic. In her youth, she was a famous European stage actress. It's said that heads of state and even royalty fell victim to her charms."

"Anyone you know?"

He gave her a disarming smile, dismissing the last of Kirsten's fears. "I've heard rumors that my grandfather fell madly in love with her and carried her picture with him to his grave."

"She's stunning. Did he ever speak of her?"

"Not to me. But I was only a boy when he died. If you like, you can ask my father about it."

"Remind me, the next time I see the king of Maurab."

Instead of laughing with her, Stefan drew a cigarette from a pack. Instantly a waiter leaned forward with a lighter. Inhaling, Stefan blew out a stream of smoke. His eyes narrowed. He should tell her now about the formal dinner, but he knew what her reaction would be. He wanted this evening to be relaxed. He needed more time. Later he would find the perfect moment to tell her about his father's . . . invitation.

"But what do you think the author was really saying?"

Stefan paused while Kirsten slipped off her other sandal.

Holding them in one hand, she caught his arm and stepped barefoot onto the sandy shore. "Obviously he wanted us to write our own ending."

"And how did you see the story ending?"

"The hero and heroine were heading for disaster."

Stefan stopped in his tracks. "Nonsense. Don't you see? They were destined to be together. Nothing would ever be strong enough to come between them."

"Stefan. She was from the planet Olny. He was an earthling. To make matters worse, their two worlds were about to go to war. They were typical star-crossed lovers, destined to have their hearts broken."

"All the more reason for them to find happiness." After reaching into his breast pocket, he held a gold lighter to his cigarette. In the flame's brief light, she saw his proud profile, the slight flare of his nostrils. He snapped the lighter shut. As they were thrust back into darkness, he exhaled a stream of smoke and said, "It will fall to these two lovers to bring their worlds back from the brink of insanity. That's the wonderful thing about people from two such diverse cultures.

Together they will form a better world for all people."

"Are you sure we read the same book?"

The rich sound of her laughter whispered over his nerves, and he dropped his arm around her shoulders, drawing her closer. "Kirsten, I can't believe you're such a pessimist."

"I prefer to think I'm a realist."

"You can have your realism. I've decided I like my ending better than yours. The hero and heroine find true love, and live happily ever after."

"Dreamer."

He turned her in his arms. "Every time I look at you, I think I'm dreaming. If I hadn't met you, I would have had to invent you." He ran his thumb over her lower lip and felt the slight trembling his touch caused. "Do you know how long I've waited to meet someone who reads the same books as I, shares the same interests?" He bent his head, brushing his lips softly over hers. Against her mouth he murmured, "Someone who would dare to argue with me?

"You make me think. You make me feel." His lips nuzzled hers. "You make me want." He crushed her to him, taking the kiss deeper.

The words she was about to speak dissolved. All thought fled. She was aware of heat, burning, searing heat as his lips moved, warm and sure over hers.

Locked in his arms, she swayed against him. Excitement ignited little fires wherever he touched her. He ran a fingertip along her silk-clad back. She could nearly feel the sparks leaping from his fingers to her body. His hands moved lower, to draw her hips firmly against his. Hearing her quick intake of breath, he drew her even closer until their bodies seemed like one.

Her form fitted his perfectly. It was as if she were the missing piece to an unfinished puzzle. Holding her, loving her, was as natural to him as breathing. He longed to know everything about her—what she thought, her favorite color, the foods she ate. He was desperate to know her body as intimately as he knew his own. He wanted to laugh with her, fight with her... wake with her beside him.

Stefan was stunned at the depth of the feelings that welled inside him. He wanted her, wanted her as he'd never wanted anyone. But at the same time he felt a fierce protectiveness. He wanted to shield her from anything that might harm her.

She felt the change in him. Almost harshly his lips plundered hers. Pulling her roughly against him, he wound his hands in her hair.

There was something different about this kiss. Though she had sensed the passion that simmered below the surface, Stefan had always managed to control it. Now it seemed to have boiled over, surprising both of them with its intensity.

"Stefan." Taking a step back, she pushed against his chest.

In the moonlight, his eyes glittered with emotion. Catching a wisp of her hair, he wound it around his finger, all the while staring down into her eyes.

"All night you've been edgy," she whispered as he lowered his mouth to hers. "At first I thought I was imagining it. Now I'm certain.'

"I'm hungry," he muttered, pressing open-mouthed kisses to her throat.

She shivered and tried to draw away, but he held her fast.

"You just had dinner."

"It isn't food I hunger for."

At her throaty laugh, he nibbled her earlobe and heard the chuckle become a little moan of pleasure. As she wound her arms around his neck, his hands moved up her sides until his thumbs found the soft swell of her breasts. He stroked and felt her body respond.

He heard her gasp and his lips covered hers, swallowing her protest. Then he crushed her against him.

She was caught up in the swirl of a passion that left her breathless and out of control. It would be so easy to give in to the weakness that was robbing her of the strength to think, to fight, even to stand. Her legs were rubber. Even as she clung to Stefan's strength, she tried to block out the passion that raged inside her. Desperately she tried to focus on one fact. She had to be strong enough to resist. Because if she gave in to her desire, she would lose herself to this overpowering man.

With a last surge of strength, she surfaced and struggled for the breath to speak. Her throat was parched. Her mouth was so dry that it hurt to form the words. "I want to go back to my villa now."

Stefan stood very still, feeling the trembling she couldn't hide. Her own pulse was none too steady.

"You can't keep trying to deny what we both know."

Touching a finger to his lips to silence him, she shook her head. "Don't speak. Just walk with me, Stefan."

As they turned back toward her villa, she glimpsed the figures on the hill. It was odd how easily she had come to accept the presence of his men.

As they approached the front door, she whispered, "Dinner tonight was wonderful. And you were right. I liked Marcella."

Beside her, Stefan was silent.

"I've made you angry."

He touched the back of his hand to her cheek. "You could never make me angry."

"Really? Even when I disagree with you about the ending of your favorite book?"

He chuckled, and the warmth of the sound enveloped her. "You might exasperate me. You might even try my patience to the very limit. But you could never make me angry."

"Good. Then I suppose this is the perfect time to tell you about all your faults. You're arrogant, spoiled, and..."

"Did I just say you could never make me angry?" She laughed as he caught her roughly by the arm. "I lied," he growled.

"There. Another fault of yours."

She saw laughter come into his eyes. In the next instant, he sobered. "There is something I have to tell you, Kirsten. I've been waiting for the right time. But there doesn't seem to be a right time. So I must tell you now."

"You look so worried."

"I don't think you're going to like it."

"Really?" She tried to make herself look properly serious, and failed. With a laugh, she said, "All right. Just tell me."

"My father has invited you to a formal dinner tomorrow night."

Her smile fled. "I don't understand."

"My father..."

"I heard you. How does he know about me?"

"He has his ways."

"You didn't tell him?"

Stefan shook his head. "I wasn't ready to...share you with my family just yet."

"Then tell him I won't be able to make his formal dinner."

"You don't understand. When my father requests something, it's actually a royal command. You can't refuse."

"But I can't go to the palace."

"Why?"

She stared up at him, her eyes suddenly wide with fear. "I don't belong in a palace. I...don't have anything proper to wear. And I wouldn't know how to behave."

"You wear the same clothes you wear with me. And just be yourself. My father isn't a fool. He'll accept you just the way you are."

"I can't. I won't. I don't believe you're even asking this of me."

His voice grew soothing. "I'm not asking you to go to the gallows for me, Kirsten. I'm simply asking you to come to dinner."

"I need time to think."

"Fine. You can have the whole day. But tomorrow night, I'd like you to be my guest."

He saw the desolation in her eyes. "Kirsten."

She looked up.

"My father would also like you to have drinks with the family before dinner."

"The family?"

He nodded.

"So they can look me over?"

She could hear the smile in his voice. "There's nothing to be afraid of. It's only my sister, the wicked witch, my brother, the mad executioner, and my youngest brother, the evil vampire. And of course, my father, the cruel king who beheads beautiful maidens."

Despite the fear that threatened to constrict her throat, she was forced to laugh. "I can hardly wait. Now you've guaranteed that I won't sleep a wink tonight."

As she turned toward the door, he caught her by the shoulders and drew her close. Brushing his lips lightly over hers, he whispered, "I could help you get through the night."

"I'll bet you could." With a quick touch of her lips to his, she hurried inside. In the darkened doorway she turned to him. He heard the slight quaver in her voice. "I don't think I can do it, Stefan. As much as I'd like to, I just don't think I'm ready to meet your family."

There was no denying the note of resignation in his voice. "You have no choice, Kirsten. My father's mind is made up. And there is one thing you must accept. The king of Maurab will not be disobeyed.''

He covered her hand with his. It was cold, and he noted a slight trembling that she couldn't hide.

''It will be fine, Kirsten. Try to sleep now.''

She nodded and allowed her gaze to linger a moment longer on his handsome face, as if to reassure herself.

She closed the door and leaned weakly against it, feeling the trembling begin in her legs. Oh, no. There was only one fact she was certain of. There would be no sleep for her tonight.

Chapter Seven

With a light blanket over her shoulders, Kirsten sipped coffee and watched the dawn gradually sweep away the darkness. A faint gray on the horizon slowly became blue sky and shimmering golden waves, until the sun burst over the eastern sky. The cool chill of night was replaced by radiant warmth.

The night had seemed interminable. Images of a stern king and angry, disapproving relatives had flitted through Kirsten's mind, jolting her awake each time she drifted off to sleep. In her dreams, she'd been dressed in rags. At the table, she'd spilled wine on the king's spotless uniform. Even the palace staff had sniffed their disappointment in the crown prince's choice of partner for the evening. The dreams were a torment, but her thoughts on awakening weren't much better.

What would she wear? She'd brought nothing appropriate for dinner with royalty. In fact, she didn't own anything grand enough. What would she talk about? These were jet-setters, accustomed to worldly people. Her little world began and ended in Fairfield, Ohio. How would she act at dinner? What if they served something completely unfamiliar to her? Would she even know how to eat it?

Letting the blanket slide to the floor, Kirsten strode to the patio and began to pace. There was no way she could deal with this. Stefan would have to accept her decision to refuse the king's invitation.

The shrill ringing of the telephone startled her. Squaring her shoulders, she hurried inside.

"Kirsten. How did you sleep?"

The mere sound of Stefan's voice weakened her resolution. How could she tell him what she'd decided? "Badly."

His tone grew more worried. "I wish I could be with you today to reassure you. But I'm afraid it's out of the question. I have to be present with my father to greet the Duke and Duchess of Kentshire. If I'm not there, they'll be hurt."

She sighed. "I understand. But, Stefan, I've decided—"

"Don't. It's all been decided for you. No matter how reluctant you may be, I want you with me tonight. I'll come by for you around seven."

Before she could protest, she heard a soft click and the line went dead.

Kirsten swam until she thought she'd drop from exhaustion. Afterward, she drifted into a deep, dreamless sleep. When she awoke, the sun was high in the sky. The morning had vanished. Not so her fears. If anything, she was even more fearful as the day moved inevitably toward night.

Going through her closet, Kirsten tried each outfit, then discarded it. Nothing was right. Brushing her hair, she tried curling it, braiding it. As her nerves grew more taut, her fingers refused to obey her commands. At last, with a cry of defeat, she fell on the bed, fighting the tears that threatened.

Her hair was a mess. She had nothing appropriate to wear to a royal dinner. She would have to refuse the king's command.

The knock on her door was a surprise. She hadn't ordered room service. Pulling on a silk wrap, she hurried to the door.

She blinked at the vision of a lovely young woman in a perfectly tailored pink suit. The girl was stunning, with small, even features and dark silken hair, which fell in a pageboy to her shoulders.

With a smile, she lowered the hand poised to knock a second time. "Kirsten?"

"Yes." She returned the young woman's probing stare.

"My name is Alana. Alana Larousse. I'm Stefan's sister."

Of course. Now she noticed that the girl had Stefan's wide, sensual mouth, the same warm smile. Clasping her extended hand, Kirsten gave her a puzzled grin. "How nice to meet you. Would you like to come in?"

The girl laughed as she stepped inside. "Stefan was in a terrible temper this morning. I think it's a case of nerves." She glanced up, her dark eyes flashing behind a thick fringe of even darker lashes. "How are your nerves, by the way?"

Kirsten gave a self-conscious laugh. "Terrible. I don't think I can handle this."

"Of course you can. That's why I came." At Kirsten's arched eyebrow, she added, "To offer my help."

"I don't understand."

"You're here on vacation," Alana said kindly. "I can imagine how disorganized you must feel. I'm only home for a few weeks myself."

"Stefan told me you attend the Sorbonne."

Alana nodded. Diplomatically she said, "I realize one doesn't pack for royal dinners while on vacation. I thought you might be able to borrow something of mine." She studied the slim figure of the woman who was causing her brother such worries. "Now that I've seen you, I'm sure you can wear my clothes."

Kirsten began to shake her head. "I couldn't possibly..."

"You must. For Stefan's sake, as well as your own peace of mind. Also I have a hairdresser coming this afternoon." Almost shyly, Alana reached out a hand to Kirsten's mane of blond hair. "He'll enjoy creating something special with such beautiful hair." Her eyes met Kirsten's. "Please say you'll let me help. It will mean so much to me. And to Stefan."

Kirsten warmed to this girl instantly. "How can I ever thank you?"

"No need for thanks. Just say you'll come with me now."

Laughing, Kirsten said, "Give me a few minutes to dress. I'll be more than happy to let you take over."

While she moved about the bedroom, she saw the young woman walk to the patio. Stefan's sister. As kind as she was beautiful. Could the rest of his family be as special?

The chauffeured limousine drove slowly through the streets of Maurab. Uneasily Kirsten glanced at the imposing palace that loomed at the top of the hill.

Seeing the direction of her glance, Alana smiled. "When I'm at school, I miss home terribly."

"Home." Kirsten shook her head. "It's hard to think of that monument as a place where a family actually lives."

"It's the only home I've ever known."

Kirsten turned to study the young woman beside her. Alana had spent a lifetime in this sunny country, behind the walls of a palace. Did she have any idea of the world beyond? Though she didn't look much like a princess, wealth and breeding were evident in the way she carried herself, in the way she wore her clothes, even in the cultured tone of her voice. But, like her brothers, she was being educated abroad. How frightening it must be to leave the security of this place for an insecure, troubled world.

The car approached the vine-covered walls that surrounded the palace. Despite the glorious array of flowers spilling over the stucco walls, Kirsten saw the glint of sunlight on electrical wire. This place was actually an impenetrable fortress.

At a small guard station, the car stopped, then continued on through slowly opening gates. As they passed, the armed guards saluted.

The car followed a wide paved road for nearly a mile before it turned into a curving driveway. Up close, the palace was a riot of formal gardens and exotic trees. As she stepped from the limousine, Kirsten tried to see this elegant setting as Stefan's home.

They climbed wide marble stairs, and then Kirsten followed Alana through double doors, where they were formally greeted by a uniformed butler. Alana led the way up a curving stairway to the second floor. At every step there were portraits of elegant women and handsome, bearded men in braid-trimmed military uniforms. Everywhere, Kirsten noted, the floors gleamed with polish, and the crystal glistened in the sunlight streaming in through high, wide windows. Along the arched walls of the second floor hallway were rich tapestries depicting the mountains and forests that surrounded this ancient village.

They entered a private suite of rooms carpeted in white and gold. There was a sitting room with delicate floral-printed sofas and mirrored tables. The bedroom was an immense room with a canopied bed and floor-to-ceiling windows that opened onto a balcony. One side of the room was dominated by a white granite fireplace. Drawn up on either side of it were gold and white love seats. Draped across foot rests were delicately embroidered throws of white cashmere shot with gold thread.

As Alana led her guest into the huge room that served as her closet, Kirsten gave a gasp of surprise.

"Take your pick."

Kirsten had never seen so many clothes outside of a department store. There were row after row of gowns, each covered in plastic, each tagged with the date it was last worn. Shelves held hundreds of pairs of shoes. There were hats and gloves for every outfit. On another rack were furs, ski jackets, raincoats, short coats, long ones.

"You must be joking. I couldn't possibly choose."

"Then I'll choose for you."

As Alana went through the rows of gowns, she paused, shook her head, then paused again.

"This one." She had selected a gown of palest shell pink silk, with a softly draped neckline and long, tapered sleeves. The bodice was covered with seed pearls and glittering amethysts. "See if these shoes fit," she offered, handing a pink sandal to Kirsten.

Kirsten slipped her foot inside and wriggled her toes. "Perfect."

"Now try the gown."

As Kirsten slipped her clothes off, Alana lifted the gown over her head and slid the silk onto her shoulders.

"Not bad. A little tuck here," she said, pulling in the waist. "A maid can do that in no time."

There was a knock on the door, and Alana admitted a smiling young man and his assistant.

"Kirsten, this is Molnar, my hairdresser, and Katie. She'll wash and dry your hair, while Molnar does mine. Then he'll find the perfect hairstyle for you."

While Alana was speaking, the young man began running a comb through Kirsten's locks. "Wonderful. Your hair is your crowning glory. I can't wait to do it."

Alana gave Kirsten a wink, then allowed herself to be led to an adjoining room, where he began washing her hair. Kirsten followed, wondering if this whole day was nothing more than a dream.

It was almost dusk, that quiet time between day and night when the air stills, and all the world seems to hold its breath.

Alana waited while Kirsten dabbed the final touches of makeup on her eyes. Turning, Kirsten paused in silence as the young princess inspected her. She could hardly wait for the final verdict.

"Oh Kirsten," the young woman breathed. "Wait until Stefan sees you. If he hasn't fallen in love already, he will tonight."

"You're exaggerating, but thank you." Walking closer, Kirsten reached for her hand. "Alana, there's no way I can ever thank you enough for what you've done today. Just the thought of this dinner had me in a panic. But now, after spending the day with you, hearing about your family, I think maybe, just maybe, I can make it through the evening."

"I know you can. You're going to have a wonderful time."

Kirsten thought about all the things Alana had told her. She'd looked through old albums at the family of adorable, laughing children. She'd stared in awe at the wedding pictures of Alexander and Anne Marie. She'd heard about the time when Stefan and Andrew had tossed a coin to see which one would get to take a famous European model to a state dinner. She'd roared in delight at the stories of Michael's escapades on the royal yacht. Thanks to Alana's hilarious stories about their childhood, Kirsten had begun to see them as a real family, not a royal one.

At a knock on the door of her suite, Alana explained, "I left word with Stefan's valet that you were here. Are you ready to see him?"

Almost shyly, Kirsten nodded. As the door opened, she felt her heart begin to race.

Stefan, dressed in a formal tuxedo with white ruffled shirt and black cummerbund and bow tie, stood quietly in the doorway. His eyes went instantly to the vision in pink. Looking from one to the other, Alana quietly let herself out. Her job was done. These two had no further need of her.

"My God. You look..." He swallowed. "Wonderful is too inadequate."

"Thank you. It was your sister's doing. She came to my villa this morning and coaxed me into letting her take over." Kirsten laughed lightly. "Thank goodness I had the sense to say yes."

"I owe her."

Kirsten moved a step closer, feeling the magnetic pull of his gaze. "So do I. How was your visit with the duke and duchess?"

"Long. Dull. I wanted to be with you. And your day?"

"Wonderful, after Alana rescued me. Until then, I thought about running away and hiding somewhere."

"I knew you'd be nervous. Kirsten, I'm sorry I let you down."

"Don't be silly." She touched a finger to his lips, and he caught her hand roughly and brought it to his mouth. "You have your duties. I understand."

"Do you?" His eyes were steady as they met hers. "Can you understand what I have to do?"

She met his look calmly. "I think so. I know that you would have been with me today if you could."

Still holding her hand, he drew her closer, until his lips hovered over hers. His warm breath feathered the little tendrils of hair that drifted from the elegant knot Molnar had fashioned atop her head.

"You look even more beautiful than I remembered." Reaching into his pocket, he said, "I brought you something."

Staring at the tiny gold box in his hand, she whispered, "You can't keep bringing me a gift each time you see me."

"Why not?"

"Because it isn't done. Besides, you'll spoil me." Before he could respond, she took the gift from his hand and lifted the lid.

He watched as her surprise slowly turned to amazement. Lifting wide eyes to him, she gasped, "Stefan. It's so beautiful."

Nestled in velvet was a tiny jeweled butterfly. Its wings were a mosaic of precious gems that gleamed in the lamplight.

"It reminded me of you. My beautiful butterfly. I had to buy it for you."

"But it's too expensive."

"Kirsten." He touched her lips to still her protest. "It could never belong to anyone else. It was made for you alone."

Gently he pinned the butterfly on the bodice of her gown. As his fingers brushed the soft swell of her breasts, she felt tiny flutterings deep inside. Glancing up, she saw him studying her closely, and knew that he had noticed the flush that stole up her throat and colored her cheeks.

"Come." He brushed his lips gently over hers. "It's time to meet the rest of my family."

"Oh, Stefan," she breathed, holding his hand tightly. "Stay close to me tonight."

He glanced down and drew her to his side. "I can't think of anyplace else I'd ever want to be."

Alana smiled as her father lit another cigarette. He was almost as nervous as the young woman she'd just left. Stefan had been a bundle of nerves, as well. The only one among them, in fact, who seemed oblivious to the upcoming meeting was Michael. Her youngest brother sat in the corner, studying the chessboard.

Andrew entered, his cuffs unbuttoned and his tie askew. At the sight of him, the king frowned. "Where's your valet? He should have seen to you before he let you out of his sight."

"I sent him away. He's always hovering. Here," Andrew said, thrusting his arm at his sister. "Do something with these cuffs."

"Drew," she said, ducking her head to hide her laughter, "you're a mess. I pity the poor woman who gets stuck with you."

"I'll leave the woman problems to Stefan. I have too many other things to worry about." When she motioned for his other arm, he turned to accommodate her.

"Such as?"

"I'm leaving for New York next week. I have a speech to memorize. I can't decide what to take and what to leave. I still have that hospital visit, unless I can get Stefan or Michael to stand in for me, and I'm scheduled to fly the new F-15 fighter plane before I leave."

"About your qualifying flight . . ."

The king looked up sharply as the door to the library opened. All eyes turned to the couple in the doorway. With his hand lightly under her arm, Stefan led Kirsten toward the king.

"Father, this is Kirsten Stevens."

King Alaric nearly dropped his cigarette. Luckily a member of the staff was at his elbow with a silver ashtray. No wonder his son had been acting so strangely lately. This woman was absolutely stunning.

"Miss Stevens."

She bowed her head as Alana had taught her, then curtsied gracefully. "Your Majesty."

When the king surprised her by extending his hand, she offered hers. He brushed his lips lightly over the backs of her fingers. Looking up, she found herself staring into piercing dark eyes.

For a long moment the king seemed lost for words. Clearing his throat, he asked, "How long have you been in our country, Miss Stevens?"

"Just a few days."

"And how do you like it?"

She felt the curious stares of the others. "I've fallen in love with your beautiful country."

He smiled then, and she realized how handsome he was. He was much younger than she would have expected. No more than fifty-five.

Offering his arm, he led her to the others. "Miss Stevens, this is my son Andrew."

The gray eyes that met hers danced with amusement. "Hello, Miss Stevens. May I call you Kirsten?"

"Of course, Andrew."

"Call me Drew. Everyone in the family does."

"Your tie's crooked," Stefan muttered beside him.

"Alana's fault. I asked her to pull me together."

Stefan shook his head and glanced from his brother to Kirsten. "Can't even be trusted to knot a tie, and he wants us to trust him with the new F-15s."

At Kirsten's raised eyebrow, the king explained, "High-altitude fighter planes." To his son, he added, "I hope you have someone going through the pre-flight list with you. You'll never remember to push all the right buttons on the instrument panel."

"Jealous," Andrew whispered to Kirsten. "Both of them jealous. Father, because he isn't licensed for jets yet. And Stefan because his boats don't have the power of my planes."

"My father was a pilot," Kirsten said softly.

"Really? Jets?"

She nodded. "But his real love was a small restored glider. He used to demonstrate it in air shows."

Stefan listened in amazement. This was the first time he could recall Kirsten volunteering anything about her family.

The king interrupted. "This is my youngest son, Michael."

The boy grinned at Kirsten. "Hello. Do you play poker or gin rummy?"

"Both."

"Great. We'll have to play a few hands."

"Watch him," Stefan warned. "His favorite hobby is playing cards with the staff. For money, of course."

Michael gave his brother a wry smile. "Now you've spoiled my scheme. Do you play chess, by any chance?"

"I'm afraid I'm quite an amateur."

"That's even better. Then I'm a guaranteed winner. If the company gets too boring after dinner, sneak in here. The board is always set up in the corner."

She glanced at the ornate board and beautifully crafted chessmen. "Oh, how lovely."

As she walked closer, Michael beamed. "I carved them myself."

"You're a sculptor?" Kirsten lifted a knight and ran a finger over the exquisite piece.

"I've done a little. My first love is portraits."

"An artist." Kirsten's smile grew. "I'd love to see some of your work."

"I'd like to show you my studio sometime." He cast a quick glance at his oldest brother. "That is, if we can pry you away from Stefan long enough."

The king put his arm around his daughter. "I understand you two young ladies have become good friends this afternoon."

Kirsten shared a secret smile with the young princess. "Alana took me under her wing. I think I would have flown away if she hadn't."

"Alana has her mother's goodness," the king said, kissing her forehead. He straightened and took a crystal glass from a serving tray.

The others followed suit.

"How long will you be in Maurab?" the king asked.

"Until the end of next week."

"So little time?"

"I have to get back to my pupils."

The king brightened. "You teach?"

"Second grade."

"And do you like it?"

Kirsten's eyes sparkled. "I love the children."

The king took a seat in an overstuffed chair drawn up by a crackling fire. The others moved to high-backed chairs that had been arranged in a semicircle.

He glanced first at Stefan, and then at the young woman at his side. "My wife was a pediatric nurse. Like you, she loved children."

"A nurse?" Kirsten couldn't hide her surprise. "She wasn't born to royalty?"

"Breeding," the king mused aloud. He turned to give Kirsten a thorough appraisal.

As Kirsten swallowed nervously, he added softly, "I knew she and I could raise nothing but Thoroughbreds."

Kirsten wasn't certain how to take the king's comment. With a shy glance at Stefan, she saw the look in his eyes and quickly turned away.

From his vantage point, the king watched the young woman who had bewitched his son. She was nervous—her hand shook slightly as she held her glass. But determined—she kept her chin up, her spine straight. She was a scrapper. He liked that. This was going even better than he'd planned.

The doors to the library opened silently. A man in formal attire announced the arrival of the first guests. Draining his glass, the king handed it to a hovering waiter and stood.

"Come, Alana. You and I will lead the way to the solarium."

Behind him, Stefan caught Kirsten's hand. Bringing up the rear were a teasing, laughing Andrew and a smug teenage Michael.

He'd been right to demand this introduction, the king thought, studying Stefan's and Kirsten's linked hands. There was no denying what his oldest son felt for the young woman beside him. It looked as though Stefan would be the first, the first since Alexander to lose his head over a beautiful woman.

She seemed nice enough. But if she was ever going to make a place for herself in this family, she'd need a whole lot more than a pleasant personality. The woman who captured Stefan's heart had better have brains, a sense of humor and the inner strength of ten people. Before the night was over, he would have a good idea of how she handled herself in the company of royalty.

Chapter Eight

The solarium was adjacent to an enclosed pool on the southern side of the palace. Clutching Stefan's arm as she entered, Kirsten halted to admire the beauty of the room. With a smile of pleasure, he watched her reaction.

Arched glass windows offered a magnificent view of the rocky cliffs and serene ocean. Exotic plants bloomed everywhere: orchids, tiny hybrid roses, creamy gardenias. Their fragrance perfumed the air. The rosy glow of a glorious sunset poured through skylights, adding to the bright, airy atmosphere. Comfortable wicker furniture and glass-topped tables invited relaxation.

"My mother had this room built when we were children. It was a place where we could all come together for fun. Before long, it became the favorite meeting room of all our friends, as well.''

"I can understand why," Kirsten said. Suddenly the palace seemed less imposing. And Kirsten found herself admiring the woman who had turned this formal residence into a real home, and forever left her imprint on it.

"I think I would have liked your mother," she whispered.

"And she would have loved you." Taking her hand, Stefan led her to the far side of the room, where the others were waiting.

Within minutes of the arrival of the royal family, guests began filling the room. As each passed through the receiving line, Kirsten was formally introduced. Stefan stood beside her, at times taking her hand in his as if to share his strength. She was grateful for his casual confidence. From every part of the room she could feel curious stares and knew that she was the object of much speculation.

"The man speaking to my father is the head of the Bank of Switzerland, Yves Montrose. His wife was once a celebrated ballerina.''

Kirsten nodded, recognizing them from news items. Taking a deep breath, she smiled and accepted their greetings.

"The rather gloomy-looking fellow leaning heavily on the cane is my father's former Minister of the Interior, Henri Soulier.''

"Former?''

Stefan's tone lowered. "Father found some . . . discrepancies in the records. He was given a promotion to a less sensitive position."

"A promotion?"

Stefan gave a mirthless smile. "Father didn't want to disgrace Henri. He's a distant cousin, as well as a boyhood friend of my father's. Although Soulier is no longer privy to confidential information, he continues to be highly visible."

Kirsten felt a chill as the object of their discussion was introduced. Beside her, Stefan was formal and correct. No one watching could have detected anything but cordiality between them.

Before long, her head began to swim with the names and faces of people she had previously only read about.

"The Duke and Dutchess of Kentshire," the butler intoned.

The white-haired duke was tall and broad shouldered. Instead of the usual black tie, his tie and cummerbund were blue-and-green tartan. Around his eyes were deeply etched laugh lines.

His wife was a willowy, silver-haired beauty, whose silver lamé gown accentuated her slender figure. The diamonds at her throat and ears added to her shimmering elegance.

Kirsten braced herself for further scrutiny. Instead, as she was introduced to the duke, she found herself caught in a great bear hug.

"So this is the one."

Beside her, Stefan grinned.

"The one?" As Kirsten recovered her composure, she glanced from the duke to his chic, perfectly turned out wife.

"Today at lunch Marcella told us all about you," the duchess said, smiling. "She made some...interesting predictions. She positively raved. And I must say, for a change, she wasn't exaggerating. In fact," the older woman told Stefan, "Marcella didn't do her justice. She's lovely."

"Thank you," Stefan replied, kissing the duchess's cheek, "almost as lovely as my favorite uncle's wife."

"Watch out for this charmer." With a little laugh of pleasure, the duchess moved on to greet Andrew, who stood beside Kirsten, and finally to hug Michael, who stood at the end of the receiving line. Kirsten could hear the roar of laughter from the duke and duchess as they greeted the wise-cracking youngest member of the family.

Turning to Stefan, Kirsten whispered, "They seem to adore your family."

"Uncle James, the duke, has been one of my father's best friends since they were boys. He and Aunt Beatrice, the duchess, were devoted to my parents. I know they grieved as much as we over the death of my mother. And they've always taken a personal interest in each of us."

When the last of the guests had been greeted, the king led the way to the dining room. Kirsten found herself seated to the king's left, beside the Duke of Kentshire.

As he held her chair, Stefan brushed his lips over her temple and whispered, "Relax. You're among friends.

My father seems to be in a festive mood. The conversation should prove to be lively."

Kirsten felt little tremors go through her body the moment Stefan touched her. When she looked up into his eyes, she saw that he was affected, too. His fingers tightened on her shoulder for a moment. Then he left to find his own place across the table.

While white-coated waiters poured wine, Kirsten thought about her disturbing dream and took a deep breath to calm herself. The last thing she needed was to spill a drink on the king and make a spectacle of herself.

There were endless toasts, to the king, to the duke and duchess, to the good people of Maurab. Without warning, Andrew offered a toast to "the lovely lady from America who graces us with her presence." While she sat blushing, the assembled crowd drank to her health. Glancing across the table, she saw Stefan wink. Her heart leaped to her throat, where it seemed lodged so often these days. She smiled, then stared down at her plate. Beside her, the king looked from one to the other. Wearing a satisfied smile, he gazed down the long table until his eyes came to rest on his youngest son. He nodded his head slightly, as if to say that Michael had won his wager, and continued eating.

"What do you do in America, Kirsten?" the duchess asked.

"I teach second grade."

"Ah. A teacher." The duchess gave her an encouraging smile. "It takes a rare gift to work with small children."

"I consider it an investment. My future will be in their hands."

"Well said," the duke commented. "We need more people who will invest wisely. Don't you agree, Montrose? Maybe the Swiss banks should solicit accounts from schoolchildren."

"Often the children are wiser than their parents." The banker turned to his wife. "Carolyn has been thinking of opening a school of ballet for the very young. She herself fell in love with the dance before she could even read or write. And she's concerned that too many little ones are pushed too hard, too soon, by their families. She would like to introduce them gradually to the rigors of dancing."

His wife nodded and addressed Kirsten. "Perhaps later this evening you would take the time to discuss your teaching methods with me, Miss Stevens. Though I know all about ballet, I have a lot to learn about teaching the very young."

Kirsten's voice warmed. "I'd love to talk with you. I saw you perform once in Chicago. You were wonderful. You have so much you could give children."

The older woman beamed at the unexpected compliment. "That was many years ago."

"I've never forgotten it," Kirsten said with feeling.

The king watched the exchange in silence. This young woman had a warmth, an openness, that endeared her even to this company of sophisticates.

Beside her, the Duke of Kentshire said, "The king is also interested in education. He is responsible for the fine university here in Maurab."

"Stefan showed it to me yesterday." Kirsten turned to the king. "He told me how you managed to lure respected professors from all over the world to join the staff. You must be very proud."

The king lifted an eyebrow in surprise. "I'm very pleased. Just how much of our country have you managed to see?"

"Only the city, so far. But I hope to take in the countryside before I leave."

"I warn you," the king said softly. "You'll fall in love and never want to leave."

"The country was my downfall," the duchess interjected. "Once I saw James's villa, I knew I had to make it my home."

"Where was your home before that?" Kirsten asked.

"I was an American, educated in Europe. My family had homes in New York, Rome, London. Though I was comfortable everywhere, I never seemed to belong anywhere. I had no roots. Since I first came here, this has been home."

"Beatrice is one of Maurab's leading citizens," the king said, giving the duchess a tender smile. "With my wife gone, and Alana at school in Paris, the duchess graciously fills in when a woman's touch is needed."

"This family definitely misses a woman's touch," the duchess said gently. Seeing the trace of pain in the king's eyes, she quickly added, "But it's only for a little while. You'll see," she said to Alana, "your years at the Sorbonne will fly, and you'll be back with your father to assume your duties."

As everyone smiled their agreement, Kirsten glanced up to see Henri Soulier staring at her thoughtfully. Seeing her look, he seemed to catch himself. Immediately he smiled and inclined his head. It happened so quickly that Kirsten found herself wondering what she'd really seen. Abruptly she dismissed the incident from her mind. These people were all friends. Good friends, who wanted only the happiness of the royal family. Still, a nagging feeling persisted. There was something in the man's eyes. Though he smiled, there was no warmth.

The waiters removed the gold-rimmed Meissen bowls that had held a clear consommé with fresh vegetables, and served the entrée, tender young duckling and truffles. Each piece of sterling silver bore the crest of the royal family. Baccarat crystal gleamed in the candlelight. Sparkling champagne was followed by dry red wine. Each course of the meal was accompanied by another wine. Kirsten was careful to take only the smallest taste of each.

While she savored dinner, Kirsten was dazzled by the opulence around her. This couldn't be happening to her. Any minute now, she'd wake from this dream and find herself back in her little room in Fairfield.

Across the table, Stefan sat watching her closely. He saw a slight flush spread across her cheeks as she met his gaze, and felt a familiar tightening deep inside. In the candle glow, her eyes sparkled brighter than sapphires. Her hair, piled regally on her head, was the color of aged whiskey. If he could, he realized with a shock, he'd steal her away from this stimulating company to the privacy of his own apartment. Just the thought of having her to himself started his pulse racing. His gaze trailed the delicate column of her throat and rested on the shadowed cleft between her breasts. His hand clenched. God, how he wanted her.

For dessert the chef had prepared a delicate custard glazed with raspberry liqueur and covered in fresh raspberries. With it, the waiters served a fruity, sweet wine and a selection of fragrant coffees and spiced teas.

"You haven't touched your dessert," the duke muttered to Kirsten.

"I've no room left. If I ate this every day, I wouldn't be able to walk."

"You sound like my wife. Before a meal like this, Beatrice fasts for a day. She claims it's the only way she can survive these feasts."

Kirsten cast an admiring glance at his wife's figure. "She must be doing something right."

"And so must you," the duke said with a laugh. At Kirsten's arched brow, he explained, "A certain young man can't take his eyes off you tonight. He's looking at you as if you were dessert."

Feeling her cheeks grow warm, Kirsten glanced down, completely missing the look that passed between the duke and the king.

Composing his features, the king announced, "There will be brandy and cigars in the billiard room." Turning to Kirsten, he said softly, "I'm sure that to a liberated American woman that sounds like an archaic custom." At her attempt to control her smile, he patted her hand. "I understand. My daughter thinks so, too. But it's something I learned from my father. Indulge me. Besides, we have changed the custom to include women."

"Cigars?" she chuckled.

"And pleasant conversation. And along with the brandy, we now serve afterdinner liqueurs. Afterward, there will be dancing in the music room." Louder he added, "We could all use a little exercise after that pleasant meal."

Following his lead, they adjourned to a wood-paneled room decorated with leather sofas and comfortable upholstered chairs. It smelled of lemony wood polish and rich tobacco. A man's retreat. The walls were hung with prints of English hunting scenes. As they entered, Kirsten spotted a lovely Gainsborough hanging over the fireplace. While some of the guests started a game of billiards, and others began talking among themselves, she stood studying the famous painting.

"Do you like it?"

Slowly Kirsten turned to Stefan. "Oh, it's beautiful. I've seen pictures of it. How long has it been in your family?"

"Since the late 1700s." He said it so casually, as if every family had the work of such masters hanging in its home. "Come on. While everyone is busy here, I'll show you the collection in my father's private apartment."

"He won't mind?"

"Of course not." Catching her hand, Stefan led her along a hallway to a small elevator.

When it came to a gliding stop, they stepped out onto plush, thick carpeting. Making their way along deserted hallways, they stopped before double doors.

"These are some of my favorites."

Stefan touched a button on the wall, and filtered light softly bathed the room. At another touch, tiny spotlights illuminated the works of art. Stunned, Kirsten stared at a bold, colorful Picasso, then studied the muted shades of a Renoir. In a place of honor over the mantel was a stunning Rembrandt, and on a marble pedestal stood a rare Rodin nude.

Stefan watched in silence as Kirsten moved from one piece to another. He noted the joy that lit her eyes as she studied the masterpieces.

"What must it be like to grow up owning such treasures? Do you know how rare these works of art are? Have you any idea how many art students have dreamed of one day seeing these?" She ran a finger lovingly over the sculpture. "Oh, Stefan, they're magnificent."

"I'd trade them all for a night with you."

Kirsten slowly turned. He stood by the fireplace, his hand resting lightly on the mantel. His face was in shadow.

"You must be very spoiled," she said, fighting to keep her tone light. "These things are priceless."

"I've found something more precious. I don't want to lose it." Though his lips lifted in a half smile, his voice sounded gruff.

"We'd better go."

As she turned away, he caught her by the shoulder. Holding her against his length, he pressed his lips to her hair, inhaling her intoxicating scent.

Against her ear he whispered, "I feel like a man who's discovered a hidden treasure, Kirsten. I ask only that I be left alone to stare at you. I don't want to let you out of my sight."

Kirsten felt a rush of heat at his touch. Turning in his arms, she lifted her face to his. His lips moved, warm and sure over hers, and familiar tremors raced along her spine.

They both jumped at the sound of someone clearing his throat. Michael stood just outside the doorway. With a grin, he called, "Here you are. Father sent me to find you. We're going to the music room now. You wouldn't want to miss the dancing, would you?"

"Yes."

Embarrassed, Kirsten shot Stefan a look. "Of course we wouldn't, Michael."

"I would, if I were you." The boy shrugged. "But you know Father. The family that plays together..."

"Umm." Stefan couldn't resist laughing. "You could tell him you couldn't find us."

"Stefan." Kirsten glanced from one brother to the other. "I'm sure the king has gone to a great deal of trouble to arrange this dance, and we're not going to disappoint him. Come on." Catching Stefan's hand, she led him to the door.

Michael slapped his older brother on the back. "Looks like you lose. You realize you're going to have to dance with every woman in the room. And Kirsten,'' he added, laughing, ''you'll have to dance with every man.''

''Every one?'' She stopped and stared at him in dismay. Turning to Stefan, she asked, ''Is Michael serious, or is he just teasing?''

''Serious, I'm afraid. You'll even have to dance with Count Rossi, who's almost ninety.''

''And watch out for his nephew, the one with the beard. He thinks he's a lady killer. Keep a tight grip on his hands.''

At her quick little frown of concern, Stefan kissed her cheek. ''Come on. It's time you found out that being a member of royalty isn't all fun and games. This is serious business tonight.''

With both men chuckling, Kirsten allowed herself to be led to the music room.

At exactly one o'clock, the king bade good-night to his guests. Although he was having a wonderful time, he knew that some of the older guests wanted to leave. Protocol wouldn't permit them to make an exit before the king.

As soon as he retired, Stefan caught Kirsten's hand and led her to the dance floor. She gave him a grateful smile.

''I've been dying to dance with the most beautiful woman in the room.''

''I thought you'd been doing that all night. I did see you with Lady Antonia Prescott a few minutes ago, didn't I?''

''Was I? I didn't notice. I was too busy watching you with Lord Windemere.''

"Oh, good. I'm glad you saw us. Isn't he a wonderful dancer?"

Pulling her closer, Stefan dropped his hand to her back. Against her temple he growled, "Be quiet, woman, and let me enjoy holding you."

"Very bold," she muttered, her lips just inches from his. "I can see that you're very bold and very spoiled."

Brushing his lips lightly over hers, he moved with the music, completely unaware of the others in the room. "This is going to be our last dance."

"And I thought we were so good together."

"We're getting out of here. Now that my father has gone, we're free to leave."

"Won't your guests think we're rude?"

He swung her in a graceful turn, then drew her closer. "I don't care what our guests think. I've shared you with them long enough."

Taking her hand, he began walking toward the door.

"Leaving so early?" Alana's dark eyes glittered with laughter.

"I think I've done an admirable job to survive this long."

"So you have." Her glance slid from her brother to the somewhat breathless young woman beside him. "How did you enjoy yourself?"

"I had a wonderful time." Kirsten stepped closer, then forgetting custom, hugged the young woman. "I can't thank you enough for all this. The gown, the hair, the confidence you gave me."

"I was glad to do it," Alana whispered against her cheek. "I hope I see you again."

"When do you go back to Paris?"

"Next week."

"Then I'd like to take you to lunch. It's the least I can do to thank you."

"I'd like that."

"If you two are through with your mutual admiration, I'd like to sneak out of here before anyone else stops us."

Alana gave Kirsten a final hug. "Watch out for my brother. He has a dangerous gleam in his eye."

Taking her hand, Stefan led Kirsten from the room and down a long, marble hallway. Turning abruptly, they followed another hall, then emerged through ornate double doors into the private gardens. Tiny lights twinkled from the branches of carefully pruned trees. More lights outlined brick-paved walkways. Following the sound of water, they approached a circular fountain. In the center, a spray of water cascaded over an intricate granite sculpture. Colored lights played on the spray, giving the water an ethereal glow.

Slipping off her sandals, Kirsten playfully dipped a bare foot in the cool water.

"Ooh, that's heavenly."

"Especially after dancing for hours." Following suit, Stefan removed his shoes and rolled the cuffs of his pants.

Pulling a bottle from beneath his jacket, he grinned. "I noticed you didn't drink anything this evening. So I helped myself to a bottle of champagne."

From his breast pocket he removed two long-stemmed crystal glasses. "Nothing but the finest for my lady."

Perched on the edge of the fountain, Kirsten accepted a glass while he poured a second for himself.

"You're crazy."

He smiled, then lifted his glass. "To the lady who stole all their hearts."

After drinking the toast, he bent and brushed his lips gently over hers, tasting the drops of champagne that lingered there. Sitting down beside her, he refilled both their glasses.

"I've waited all night to have you to myself."

"Do you intend to get me drunk and seduce me?"

His hand paused in midair. He studied her a moment. "Good idea. Any objections?"

"I think," she said, giggling suddenly, "that you may end up carrying me home." Standing in the pool, she kicked up a spray of water with her foot. "I feel suddenly giddy with relief that this night is over. Oh, Stefan, I want to run, I want to fly, I want to. . ."

"Swim." Standing, he caught her hand and pulled her under the cascading fountain.

The weight of the water dragged the pins from her hair and sent it streaming down her back. The once elegant gown clung to her body like a second skin.

"Oh no! Your sister's gown."

"Don't worry about it. She has so many, she can't possibly wear all of them. Besides, I'll make it up to her." He gave a snort of laughter. "She'll see to that."

Stefan's tuxedo jacket was so waterlogged that he slipped it from his shoulders. His white shirt was plastered to his chest and arms.

With the water pouring over them, they clung to each other and laughed in abandon.

"Now I know you're crazy," she said between peals of laughter.

"It's you," he chuckled, "I've always wanted to be free to do these things. With you, Kirsten, I've finally found real joy in my life. Just being here in Maurab is a wonderful adventure since I met you."

He stared down into her laughing eyes and pulled her out of the water's spray. Wiping her hair from her face, he traced the shape of her brow, the curve of her cheek, all the while staring down into her eyes.

"Kirsten. My sweet, beautiful, bewitching Kirsten."

His lips covered hers, sending shock waves of fire and ice colliding. Her body was cold from the water. Yet everywhere he touched her, she was on fire.

Putting her arms around his waist, she could only cling to his strength. His lips tasted of champagne and cold, fresh water. Moving her hands along his back, she thrilled to the ripple of muscles beneath his wet shirt.

She could feel his strength. He was a virile male animal. But he had more than physical strength. Beneath his charm, his teasing laughter, lay a core of steel. He would always be there for the ones he loved. It was something she knew without question.

He kissed her gently, almost tentatively, as if afraid to take her too far, too fast. As if, she thought, tasting the moistness of his lips, he was waiting for permission. This man, this playboy, was treating her as if this were their first kiss. She could deal with his ego, his charm, his silliness. But this, this almost fearful reverence was something new in their relationship. His unexpected sweetness was her undoing.

Feeling her gradual response, Stefan took the kiss deeper, loving the way she felt in his arms. This was what he'd waited for, yearned for. This woman. Each time he touched her, held her, he was overcome with emotion. He could understand his desire. She was a beautiful, desirable woman. What threatened to undermine his control was the need he felt. Never before had he experienced such a gnawing, almost painful, need.

His mouth was no longer gentle. His kiss became fierce. His hands, holding her firmly against him, began kneading her back.

He heard her murmur his name against his mouth. Her warm breath mingled with his, and something exploded inside him. The thin wet silk of her gown was no barrier to his hand. Finding her breast, he heard her moan, and answered with one of his own.

His hands skimmed her wet skin, feeling her heat. She strained against him, offering more. This was what he'd dreamed of, this mad, mindless hunger driving both of them to the brink.

Scooping her into his arms, he stepped over the rim of the fountain and began striding toward the palace.

With her head against his chest, she could feel the wild rhythm of his heart.

"Where are we going?"

"Where I've wanted to be all evening. To my apartment."

Her heart raced. She ought to stop him. But the truth was, she didn't have the strength. She wanted him every bit as much as he wanted her. There was no denying it.

Shoving the door open with his foot, he continued inside and climbed a flight of stairs effortlessly. At the top of the stairs he pushed open a second door, then strode through dimly lit rooms until he came to the bedroom. Only then did he pause to set her on her feet. Before she could glance around, he drew her against him and covered her lips firmly with his.

Heat flared inside her, leaving her flushed and breathless.

"Kirsten," he murmured against her mouth. He nibbled her lower lip, teasing it until she thought she couldn't wait another second. Then he stared down into her eyes. "My beautiful, beautiful Kirsten."

Her eyes widened, and he saw a dreamy softness come into them.

"Even when we're apart, I taste you," he muttered, rubbing his lips gently over hers. "You've a taste like no other, did you know?"

She blinked, and found she couldn't answer.

"I haven't decided if it's your beauty that first attracted me, or your cool arrogance," he breathed against her mouth.

"I don't care. Just kiss me," she sighed.

Still he lingered, touching, tasting, barely brushing her lips with his. She could feel her need for him growing, until she thought she would explode from wanting him.

"Maybe it's your body," he whispered, running a hand down her back. He felt her tremble at his touch.

"So perfect." The wet silk was plastered to her skin, outlining every line and curve.

Very deliberately, he traced his fingers along her hips to her narrow waist, then brought his hands higher, to cup the swell of her breasts. At her little sigh of pleasure, his eyes narrowed. His thumbs moved across her nipples, which were already erect from his touch.

"Stefan." His name was torn from her lips moments before his mouth crushed hers.

Kirsten reeled from the impact of the kiss. Never had she wanted like this. Her entire body trembled. She gave a little gasp as her tongue met his. Raw, gnawing hunger drove her. Her heartbeat roared like thunder in her temples.

His lips left hers to roam her face, pausing at the corner of her eye, her cheek, the corner of her mouth. Yet over and over again, his lips returned to her mouth, to plunder, to taste, to drink of her sweetness.

As he drove her even closer against him, Kirsten became aware of a sound—the closing of a door. Through the passion that clouded her mind, she fought to remember where she was. As his hands tangled in her hair, she stiffened slightly, remembering. His apartment in the palace. An army of servants. Bodyguards. Prying eyes.

"Stefan." Pushing against his chest, she stared up into eyes heavy lidded with emotion. "There's someone in here with us."

Cupping her face in his hands, he kissed the tip of her nose. "Probably one of the maids," he murmured. "Fetching clean linen or turning down the lights."

Kirsten took a step backward and felt his arms tighten at her waist. Lifting wide eyes to him, she whispered, "I want to leave."

"No, you don't." He brought his lips to her throat and gave a warm chuckle. "You want the same thing I do."

With a sigh of anger she pushed herself roughly from his arms. "It's obvious you and I were raised in very different cultures. To you, these people are invisible." Turning away, she added, "I can't pretend I don't see your staff. They're everywhere. And their presence is stifling."

Stefan went very still. In a low, angry voice, he asked, "Are you saying you won't stay here with me?"

"That's exactly what I'm saying. I'd like to leave. Now." She let out a long, shuddering sigh.

"And these feelings we have for each other? What do you propose we do about them?"

"Nothing." She turned to face him. "There's nothing we can do. I want to leave now."

In a tightly controlled voice, he said, "I want you, Kirsten. And you want me."

"Want. The prince of Maurab always gets what he wants, doesn't he?"

His eyes became narrow, angry slits. "Don't try to deny what we both feel."

"I'm not denying it." She took in deep gulps of air to steady her voice. "But I won't stay with you here. I want to go back to my villa. I'm...afraid."

"Why?"

"Because you're a prince."

"A man," he said with feeling.

Her voice was a cry of pain. "I know. Oh, how I know. When we're together like this, I know. At least, for a little while, I convince myself you're just a man. But don't you see, Stefan? When we're apart, I remember who you are."

Almost sadly, she added, "Tonight, I felt like Cinderella. Everything was so beautiful. But the midnight hour has arrived. I have to go back to being Kirsten Stevens from Fairfield, Ohio. And you can't help being who you are—Prince Stefan, the future king of Maurab."

He heard the pain in her voice. Dropping his hands to his sides, he muttered, "I'll send for the car."

With her sandals still dangling from her hand, she lifted her wet skirts and walked down the stairs and out the door.

As he stood in the courtyard staring after her, Stefan was reminded of the first time he'd seen her. He'd thought her a mermaid, an apparition. Someone he'd invented to ease the loneliness.

There had to be a way to convince her that they were right for each other. When she left his country—if she left, he corrected himself—the loneliness would be unbearable.

From the shadows, his bodyguards moved silently into place behind him. And in the darkness, her delicate fragrance trailed on the night breeze and disappeared. As he feared she would.

Chapter Nine

A beam of sunlight found its way through the center of the drapes, bathing the figure in the bed. For long moments Kirsten lay curled in its warmth, refusing to open her eyes. Finally, with a sigh, she gave in to the prodding of the morning and looked around.

If the wilted silk gown hadn't been hanging over the door of her closet, she might have believed that she'd imagined last night. It had been the most exhilarating night of her life. And the most heart wrenching.

She glanced at the plane ticket on her night table. Her dream vacation was quickly passing. In no time she would have to return to the world of reality. And when she did, she wanted to leave with no regrets. She would have to keep reminding herself that she'd been given a special gift. Stefan's attentions had turned this trip into something magical, something wonderful.

But this holiday romance could never stand the test of time. What made it special was the fact that they were two people from entirely different backgrounds who had forgotten their obligations for just a little while. A year from now, Kirsten thought with a sudden stab of pain, Stefan wouldn't even be able to remember her name. But she would never forget him. Or these wonderful days together.

His family had been a complete surprise. She'd expected them to be aloof or stuffy or regal. Instead, they were a real family, laughing, teasing, supporting one another. His brothers had treated her with casual acceptance. His sister had appointed herself Kirsten's protector, and had expressed real warmth and affection. Even the king had shown genuine interest in his son's friend. After her initial awkwardness, Kirsten had forgotten the fact that they were royalty. They were the sort of family she had always wished for. They were kind, and loving and surprisingly... fun.

The phone on her night table shrilled, interrupting her thoughts. Tossing aside the blanket, she reached for it on the second ring.

"Kirsten?"

Recognizing Alana's soft, cultured voice, Kirsten felt a swift rush of disappointment. She had hoped... Pushing aside her sadness, she tried to make her voice sound cheerful. "Good morning."

"I hope I didn't wake you."

Swinging her feet to the floor, Kirsten stood. "I was awake. But until now I've been feeling too lazy to get up."

"You promised me a lunch." Alana gave a little laugh. "Would I be too bold to ask what your plans are for today?"

Kirsten sank back down on the edge of the bed. If she wasn't going to be with Stefan, she couldn't think of a nicer way to spend the day. "I'd love to take you to lunch."

"Do you have any place in mind?"

Kirsten chuckled. "This is your country, not mine. I'll let you pick the spot."

"Wonderful. Why don't I come for you around eleven?"

"Fine. I'll look forward to it."

As Kirsten replaced the receiver, she swallowed back the last remnant of disappointment and hurried to find her bathing suit. There was enough time to swim before she had to shower and dress.

He didn't call. All morning she had prayed for the ringing of the phone. Even while she was swimming, she'd left the patio door ajar so that she could hear the sound of the telephone.

Hearing the sound of a car's engine and the tap tap of high heels along the walk, Kirsten gave a last glance in the mirror and hurried to open the front door.

Alana was wearing a pale blue silk suit. Beneath the jacket was a blouse of delicately embroidered blue and white. Her dark hair swung freely about her shoulders.

With a smile Kirsten motioned her inside. "I'll only be a minute. I have to find my purse."

As Kirsten rummaged through the closet, Alana paused in the doorway of the bedroom. Glancing up, Kirsten saw the puzzled look on the young princess's face as she studied the limp gown hanging over the door.

"Oh, dear. Alana, please let me explain about your dress."

"It appears you went for a swim."

"Yes. Well, not really. You see, I fell into the fountain." Seeing Alana's arched eyebrow, she tried to clarify. "Well, I didn't exactly fall. I was pushed. I mean..."

Alana could no longer keep a straight face. Bursting into laughter, she said, "You don't have to explain. I warned you about that gleam in my brother's eye, didn't I?"

Kirsten joined in the laughter. "You did. But I didn't realize just how crazy he could be. I promise you, I'll have the dress cleaned and repaired. Before you get it back it'll be as good as new."

"Don't worry." Alana turned and followed Kirsten toward the front door. "Let Stefan deal with it. He knows I'll make him replace that gown if he can't fix it."

"That's exactly what he said. But it's my responsibility. After you were so kind to lend it to me, I would feel awful if I didn't return it in perfect shape."

As they stepped outside, Kirsten glimpsed a man standing beside the car and gave an involuntary shiver.

"I'd forgotten. I'd hoped we'd be alone," she said softly.

Alana turned in time to see the look of concern on Kirsten's face. "We will be. Over lunch."

After giving directions to the driver, Alana settled back against the cushions, aware that the young woman beside her was watching the dark car that followed them. "Did Stefan call you this morning?"

Kirsten averted her gaze, staring at the passing scenery, but seeing nothing. After the argument she had started last night she had probably driven him away for good. "No. I haven't heard from him."

Though the words were spoken softly, Alana heard the underlying pain in Kirsten's voice and maintained a discreet silence for the rest of the journey.

The car stopped in front of a stunning little restaurant made almost entirely of glass. Built on a bluff, it offered an uncluttered view of the soaring mountain peaks surrounding them and the sparkling Mediterranean below.

Alana was warmly greeted by the maître d', who led the two young women to a private booth. Alana ordered a pale golden wine.

"It's a specialty of my country," she explained. "Made here in a lush green valley dotted with vineyards. If you have time, you must visit our wine country."

"There are so many things I'd like to see." Kirsten's voice was wistful. "If only there were time."

When their meal had been ordered, Alana turned toward her companion. "Stefan was up early this morning," she said casually.

Kirsten toyed with her fork. Why did the mere mention of his name tug at her heart?

"He seemed reluctant to accompany my father to a farewell brunch with the duke and duchess aboard their yacht."

"Reluctant? I thought he adored them."

"I think there were other things he would have preferred to attend to today."

Kirsten chose to ignore Alana's implication. "Why didn't you go along?"

Alana gave a knowing smile. "I thought it was the perfect opportunity to have a private little talk with you."

Kirsten's head came up. "What about?"

The princess touched Kirsten's hand in a gesture of understanding. "About you and my brother. Stefan was in a terrible mood when I saw him this morning."

Kirsten remained silent.

"Did you quarrel last night because he threw you in the fountain?'

At that, Kirsten gave a quick laugh of surprise. Shaking her head, she murmured, "That was just a silly, spontaneous act. We both laughed ourselves to tears over it." Glancing down, she added, "I could never get angry at Stefan for the crazy, funny things he does."

Alana gave a little sigh of relief. "I'm so glad." She leaned back, allowing her head to rest against the back of the booth. Staring a moment at the ceiling, she added, "I've never seen Stefan as moody as he's been since he met you. One minute he's so happy he could charm the birds from the trees. The next, he's ready to tear down brick walls with his bare hands. This is something new for Stefan." Tilting her head, she fixed

Kirsten with a steady gaze and boldly asked, "What have you done to my brother?"

For long moments Kirsten ran a finger around the rim of her wineglass, deep in thought. Finally lifting her eyes to Alana's, she said softly, "I suppose he feels I've rejected him. Or rather, his way of life."

The young woman beside her went very still. While a formally attired waiter served their meal, the two remained silent. When they were alone again, Alana carefully spread her napkin across her lap before speaking.

"Just what is it you find so repugnant about Stefan?"

"Repugnant?" Kirsten's eyes widened. How could his sister even suggest such a thing? "Stefan is the most considerate, attentive, charming man I've ever met. He makes me think, and feel, and best of all, he makes me laugh."

The smile returned to Alana's lips. "Just now, Kirsten, one would think you sounded like a woman in love."

Kirsten's smile fled. "Don't be silly. Just because I enjoy being with your brother, don't read more into it than you should. I was simply defending him. I couldn't possibly find Stefan repulsive."

"But you told me you rejected him."

"His way of life." Deliberately Kirsten took a sip of wine, then set the glass down. "I'm not accustomed to maids and drivers and . . . armed guards dogging my footsteps."

Alana's tone softened. "Not too many people are. It is a necessary part of our lives. And yet we realize it also presents a barrier. Many people, people we care about, are held at arm's length by the presence of so many attendants. My brothers have few close friends who understand their way of life. Maybe that's why our family is so close."

"And what about you, Alana?" Kirsten asked. "How do you manage to slip from the sheltered life of a princess to the casual life of a student in Paris?"

"Sometimes," Alana murmured, "I feel a little like an actress. Though I miss my home and country very much, I'm exhilarated by the sense of freedom when I'm away. At school, though my name is recognizable, there is a feeling of anonymity. No one accosts me. And I've found that most of my fellow students treat me as one of them." She spread her hands. "So for a little while, I get to pretend."

"And Stefan?" Kirsten asked. "Will he ever again be able to become anonymous?"

"Stefan." Alana's tone softened. "I'm afraid the role thrust upon him has been a burden as well as an honor. But he's a very strong man. He'll cope. I think, with time, he will slip as easily into a position of leadership as his beloved boats slip into the ocean's waves. But it would ease his burden to have someone strong beside him. Someone with whom he can relax and forget his worries." Her voice lowered. "We would all love to see him find someone he can trust completely. Someone with whom he can laugh and be himself. Tell me, Kirsten, is there someone special waiting for you in America?"

The reply was barely more than a whisper. "No. No one."

"Have you ever been married?"

Kirsten's eyebrow arched at the question. "I've never even come close to such a commitment."

"And you love children." Casting a sideways glance at the woman beside her, Alana smiled suddenly. "I think it's good we had this little talk. At least now I better understand my brother's abrupt mood swings."

"You do?" Kirsten felt even more confused than before.

Picking up her fork, Alana said, "Let's eat. The food looks wonderful."

Kirsten cast a doubtful glance at the exotic dishes. "I don't think I could eat a bite." All this talk of Stefan had left her with an empty feeling. Last night she'd ridden a roller coaster of emotions. She had angered and rejected Stefan. She had made him only too aware of their differences. And this morning, he hadn't called. Perhaps they would never see each other again. The thought caused an ache that was unexpectedly sharp.

"I was thinking that maybe after our lunch you might like to go with me to the air force test site."

"Why?"

"Andrew is flying the F-15 today."

"The high altitude fighter?"

"Oh, you remembered. Yes, he hopes to qualify before leaving for New York."

"It must be very important to him." Kirsten fought to quell the slight fluttering in her chest.

Alana nodded. "I sometimes think my brothers run faster, live harder, more on the edge, because of the role into which fate has cast them." She sighed. "I think they fantasize about being ordinary citizens, pursuing normal lives. But they've learned that they have certain duties. Regardless of personal preference, they will always do what they must.''

''I don't think I could watch. I'd be too aware of the danger.''

''Drew's a fine pilot. There's nothing to be afraid of.''

Kirsten seemed to hesitate a moment. ''Will Stefan be at the test site to watch Andrew qualify?''

''I doubt he'd miss it. He and father will probably come directly from the duke's yacht.''

For a moment her heartbeat was unsteady. She would have a chance, maybe her last, to see him at least, to be near him once more. She would ask for no more than that. No matter what the cost to her nerves.

''I think I'd like to go.'' Taking a long breath, Kirsten speared a piece of tender broccoli. ''Oh, this is wonderful. I didn't realize how hungry I was. I'm so glad you suggested lunch today.''

Alana swallowed back a laugh. Somehow, she'd known that the prospect of seeing Stefan would cause Kirsten to regain her appetite and her enthusiasm. Kirsten Stevens might be able to tell herself she was strong enough to resist Stefan, but Alana was beginning to think she knew better. There was a war of wills going on between these two people, two people she cared about very much. And she was betting on her brother. She'd never seen him so frustrated, or so determined. If Stefan played his cards right, this strong-willed woman might just lose the battle. And her heart.

* * *

All morning the sky had been a clear cloudless blue. Warm sunlight filtered through the canopy that shaded the figures on the deck of the gently rolling yacht. King Alaric and the duke were in rare form. There was an easy familiarity between the two old friends, who were completely relaxed in each other's company.

Stefan took a sip of black coffee, hoping the warmth would drive away the lingering chill of frustration. Late into the night he had paced, mulling over Kirsten's rejection. When he awoke at first light, thoughts of her nudged everything else from his mind.

While the laughter and teasing comments went on around him, he walked to the rail and watched the billowing canvas of a magnificent sailboat far from shore.

Freedom. That was what sailing meant to him. The freedom to catch the wind, to skim the waves, to leave the snug harbors behind and chart any course he chose.

Leaning a hip against the rail, he stared at the sunlit waves and thought once more about Kirsten. If only he were free to be the kind of man she wanted. He frowned against the glare of the sunlight. She deserved only the best—to be cherished by someone who could give her a life of ease, a life of complete freedom. If he, having been born to it, railed against the lack of privacy in his life, how could he expect someone like Kirsten to accept it? Hearing a raucous burst of laughter from his father, he wondered again how the overbearing king had ever managed to persuade his beautiful, headstrong mother that they could live in harmony. Was passion enough? Apparently not, Stefan thought with sudden anger, or he would have made Kirsten his on their first meeting. During that first kiss he had sensed the passion that lay smoldering just below her serenity. Was mutual need enough to form a relationship? If so, he and Kirsten would have overcome their differences already. Though she tried to conceal it, her needs were as compelling as his. How did two people from different backgrounds, different cultures, find a way to come together?

"Your food grows cold."

He turned at the sound of the duchess's soft voice beside him.

"I'm not really hungry."

"Force yourself. Otherwise, the chef will be insulted. And you know how he sulks."

Tossing down the last of his coffee, he placed a hand beneath her elbow and walked with her to the table.

The breeze ruffled the filmy sleeves of her dress. "I had hoped you'd bring Kirsten with you this morning. James and I were enchanted with her."

He forced a smile. "I didn't ask her. I thought my father and James would prefer a private visit."

"Did she enjoy the party last night?"

Stefan's hand clenched at his side. It was painful to speak of Kirsten. His emotions were too close to the surface. He fought to keep the edge from his tone. "She said she felt like Cinderella."

The duchess glanced at his face as he held her chair. Touching a hand to his arm, she murmured, "I remember feeling quite overwhelmed when James first brought me here. Even now, after all these years, I'm amazed at how much your lovely country has become like home to me."

Stefan brushed his lips across her cheek. "I can't picture you ever being overwhelmed, Beatrice."

"Then believe me." She sat quickly and unfolded her napkin. Giving Stefan a quick smile, she patted his hand. "Sometimes, when a woman is intimidated, she puts up a protective wall to keep from being hurt. Especially if she thinks things are moving too quickly." Her voice lowered. "Give it time, Stefan."

"That's a luxury I can't afford. She has very little time here."

"Time?" The king looked up from his conversation. "Is there a problem? I thought we'd have time for a leisurely brunch before we parted."

"We have plenty of time," the duke assured him. "We don't have to be in Cannes until this evening."

Beatrice smiled gently at the annoyance she could read on Stefan's face as he took a seat at the table. Even a man in his position could be unsettled when he found himself facing the uncertainties of love. And she had no doubt that he was a man in love. Perhaps a man possessed would be a better description. That beautiful young woman she had met last night was certainly the cause of his distraction today.

"I wish you could stay to watch Andrew fly," the king said to his friend.

"I have no doubt he'll be brilliant," the duke replied. "Drew was born to fly." His head came up as a sudden question occurred to him. "You aren't worried, are you?"

"Of course not. He's been flying for years. But the F-15 is a complicated piece of equipment. And Andrew does tend to be . . . careless."

"What do you think, Stefan?"

With difficulty the prince pulled himself away from his distracting thoughts of Kirsten. "When Drew climbs into the cockpit of a plane, he becomes one with it. He's as natural as a bird." With a smile he added, "Now if he were representing us in a fashion show, we'd all have to worry."

As they laughed, the duchess asked, "Will Michael and Alana be there to watch?"

The king lifted a cup of steaming coffee to his lips. "Michael assured me he wouldn't miss it." He glanced at Stefan and asked, "Did you see Alana this morning?"

Stefan shrugged. "Just in passing. She seemed rather vague about her plans."

Accepting a second helping of spinach crepes, Alaric declared, "She assured me she'd be there." He didn't bother to add the rest of what his daughter had told him. He was content with the special name he had added to the list of guests who would witness his son's flight. "This is an important day for Andrew. He'll want to share it with the people he loves. Any achievement is sweeter when shared with those we love."

Beatrice chanced a quick glance at the proud profile of the ruling monarch and then at his heir. Despite the casual tone of the conversation, she sensed some deeper meaning. What was really on Alaric's devious mind, she wondered. He was as smug as a cat toying with a mouse. She'd be willing to bet this had something to do with Stefan and his elusive lady love.

Stefan pushed his plate away and opened a gold cigarette case. As he exhaled a stream of smoke, his eyes narrowed. "How long will you be in Cannes, James?"

"Two or three weeks." The duke dismissed their waiter and drained his cup. "We thought we'd take our cue from the weather. As long as the sun continues to shine on us, we'll linger. If the sun flees, we'll go on." He looked up. "Thinking of joining us, Stefan? We'd love to have you."

The prince shrugged. "Not right now. Maybe later." When the numbness wore off and the pain set in, he'd need to get away for a while.

"Might do you good," the duke continued. "I can't remember when I've ever known you to spend so much time at home without getting restless."

The king's gaze fastened on his son's face. "Maybe Stefan's decided the grass is greener at home."

The duchess rang for their waiter, deliberately changing the direction of their conversation. "A bottle of champagne before we go."

Stefan gave her a grateful smile. "One quick toast," he said, "and then we have to leave for the airstrip. Andrew can't be kept waiting."

The car climbed steadily through lush countryside, then veered suddenly. The road had been cut through verdant hills. The pavement was new and smooth. Though there were no signs to mark the route, Kirsten knew this had to be military land. The only traffic was an occasional army vehicle. After driving for another mile, they stopped at a checkpoint. Up ahead, a car blocked their way. While they watched, the driver of the vehicle turned it around, spewing dirt and gravel as he parked it on the shoulder of the road. Alana's driver lowered his window, and a scowling Henri Soulier hurried over. Bending low, he studied the two young women in the back seat. Sweat beaded his brow and upper lip. He wiped it with a handkerchief.

"I was told I was not permitted to drive to the airstrip," he complained. "Something about needing a pass. What's going on? Why am I being barred?"

"A special flight today," Alana said softly. "I don't think Father was expecting anyone except the family."

"And what am I?"

Kirsten noted the flare of his nostrils.

"I mean immediate family, Henri. I'm sorry."

"They won't allow my car to pass. May I ride with you?"

As he lifted a hand to the door, an armed soldier stepped closer.

"I'm sorry, Princess Alana. I have a list of approved spectators. There can be no exceptions. I have already explained this to Monsieur Soulier."

Alana gave an innocent shrug. "They have their orders, Henri. If you'd like, I'll speak to my father."

"By then it will be too late."

"I'm sure he'll be here in plenty of time to permit you to view the flight."

"Much too late." With a look of fury the man turned away.

For a moment Alana watched him. Then she nodded to the driver, who expertly steered the car around the blockade and drove on.

"How was I permitted to pass?" Kirsten asked.

"I gave your name to Father this morning."

"But how could you possibly have known then that I'd be willing to come?"

"There are some things women know without asking," Alana replied.

The airstrip was built on a plateau overlooking the city. Dozens of planes and helicopters lined the runways.

Their car halted in front of the control tower, and the driver helped them out. Following a military escort, they filed through the enormous hall and up the stairs to the tower.

Inside there were fewer than a dozen people. Several men and women in military uniform clustered around the monitors, checking equipment. Standing in front of a window, the king and Michael were engaged in an animated conversation with a general. But Kirsten was aware of only one figure in the room. He had turned at the sound of their arrival. While she was introduced to the military personnel, she felt the full impact of his intense gaze focused on her. Following Alana like a robot, she greeted the other guests, then the king and his youngest son. And finally, there was only one person left to greet. Crossing the room, she stopped just an arm's length from Stefan.

Her dress was of prim navy blue, with a tailored jacket and brass buttons. Her hair had been pulled back into a tidy knot, adding to her pristine appearance. But he was aware of the perfect figure hidden beneath the dress, of pale skin that colored at his mere touch. When she walked closer, her delicate scent sharpened his senses. He schooled his features to show absolutely no emotion. His cool amber eyes were shuttered.

Feeling her throat go dry, she extended her hand, aware that everyone in the room was observing. Though her mind was in turmoil, her voice was low, controlled. With a husky whisper, she murmured, "Hello Stefan."

What he wanted to do was to crush her to him, to feel those velvet lips part beneath his, to savor her clean fresh taste. With icy calm, he surprised even himself by accepting her handshake. Despite the jolt he felt at her touch, his voice sounded cool. "How were you ever persuaded to pass through such close military inspection?"

Her laugh was a little too breathless. "Just curious," she said, "to see how the other half lives."

Chapter Ten

Stefan continued to hold her hand, unaware of the others in the room. Around him all activity seemed to grind to a halt. Voices became a muted chorus in the background. There was only this woman, this moment. He hadn't known how badly he'd wanted to see her until now. Just the sight of her eyes, wide and innocent, took his breath away.

She looked fresh and rested. While he had paced the night away, tormented by images of a lost love, she had apparently slept like a babe.

"How did you and Alana happen to arrive together?"

"Over lunch she asked me if I'd like to watch Andrew's qualifying flight."

"Lunch." Clearly he was puzzled.

"You remember. I promised Alana I'd take her to lunch to thank her for her help." Forcibly Kirsten removed her hand from his. "Your sister phoned this morning and suggested that this would be the perfect day."

"Odd. She didn't say a word about her plans to me."

"How was your brunch with the duke and duchess?"

She saw his eyebrow lift before he muttered, "Fine."

Before he could say more, Andrew's voice, amplified through a bank of speakers, interrupted the low hum of conversation.

"This is Fox One. Preflight completed. Request clearance from tower."

"Ladies and gentlemen." A dour man in military uniform called for attention. "We suggest you view the flight from the outer observation deck."

"This way." As the others began filing out, Stefan steered her toward a balcony that wrapped around the control tower.

"Andrew will take off from that runway," Stefan said, pointing to their right.

The others had already surged along the railing. Alana was clutching her father's arm. Beside her, Michael was holding a pair of binoculars. In little groups of two and three, the military personnel watched with interest. Standing slightly away from the crowd, Stefan and Kirsten had an unrestricted view of the airfield below.

The wind was stronger here, whipping at the hem of Kirsten's skirt, freeing little tendrils of hair from the knot at her nape.

"You'll want to use these," Stefan said, handing her a pair of binoculars. As he focused his on the idling plane, he added, "There's Drew. He's just fastening his helmet."

She fiddled with the glasses and felt her throat go dry. The plane was sleek and graceful, a gleaming silver. She was reminded of the planes her father had flown.

"Yes. I see him now." Sharpening the focus, she whispered, "He's waving. Stefan, I think he's waving."

At the rail, the king lifted his hand in a salute. Beside him, Michael and Alana waved at the figure outlined in the Plexiglas dome.

The aircraft began a slow, steady taxi to the end of the runway. Over an outdoor speaker, the observers could hear the controller issuing precise instructions. Andrew's responses were delivered in a monotone.

"Is he really that calm?" Kirsten whispered.

She sensed that Stefan, beside her, was straining to hear every word.

"He's so absorbed in what he's doing, he has no time for nervousness. There are a hundred details to see to before takeoff."

"You're cleared for takeoff, Fox One."

The small plane paused a few moments at the end of the runway. Then the sound of the engines increased to a deafening roar as the craft sped along the tarmac and lifted skyward.

Passing to the right of the tower, the plane continued to climb until it seemed no more than a silver bird in the heavens. Behind it a jet stream billowed, marking its path clearly in the sky. Slowly Andrew turned the craft, doubling back on his course. As he passed directly overhead, the observation deck hummed with the noise of the engines. For a moment the voice on the speaker was blurred by static. Then Andrew's words could be heard clearly by the observers.

"...a flaw in the control. Repeat, there seems to be a flaw in the control."

The careful voice of the controller never wavered. "Describe the flaw, Fox One."

"One of the monitors is not functioning. There's no way to tell whether or not the craft will accept manual directions."

The crowd on the observation deck had grown deathly silent. Kirsten was certain she could hear the pounding of her heart.

"Can you go on without the monitor, Fox One?"

She strained to hear the response.

"No problem," came Andrew's calm voice.

"All right, Fox One. The first part of the test calls for a roll maneuver."

The plane made a graceful roll in the sky, then passed loudly overhead.

"He's too low," the general said, then swore softly.

The voice of the controller interrupted. "Can you take her up, Fox One?"

All eyes focused on the silver object streaking across the sky.

"Negative. It refuses the command."

King Alaric dropped his binoculars and touched the sleeve of the general beside him. His words were spoken in a low command. "Don't take any chances."

"He's a seasoned pilot, Your Majesty." The general's tone held quiet authority.

"It's fighting me," Andrew said.

The crowd waited.

"Still won't ascend. In fact, I think I'm dropping lower. The altimeter doesn't record."

"He should eject," Kirsten snapped.

"He would have to take it out over water." Stefan's voice was low with emotion. "This is a populated area. Drew would never risk other lives."

Kirsten dared not breathe. Every part of her was straining, willing Andrew to control the aircraft. How could his family calmly watch and listen?

"There." It was Andrew's voice, showing no change from the calm, even tone he had used during the crisis. "The light's on. It will take the command now. What altitude do you request?"

"Go to forty thousand feet, Fox One."

The voices droned on, but Kirsten had already stopped hearing them. They were nothing more than a hum of sound from her past. Unaware of what she was doing, she gripped Stefan's arm.

Seeing her troubled look, he whispered, "Kirsten, what's wrong."

She brought her hands to her ears to blot out the voices. "It's all happening again."

"What is?"

"That night. The crash. Oh, Stefan, it's so terrible to be up there when everything goes wrong."

His voice lowered. "Tell me about it."

She spoke in a haunted voice. "I was nine years old. I was sitting behind my mother, who was in the copilot's seat. My father was flying us home from Chicago. The weekend in the big city had been a wonderful adventure." Her voice lowered. "At first it was raining, the kind of cold rain that spatters the windshield and slowly turns to ice." Kirsten's eyes were wide with the memory. "To stay calm, we started singing a silly little song we all knew. Then the storm began in earnest. Lightning streaked across the sky, leaving us blinded for a moment. Thunder rocked the plane. I remember trembling, holding my mother's hand. The lights in the cabin went out.

I cried out, and my father took his hands from the controls long enough to comfort me." She closed her eyes a moment. "I can still feel his big hands around my small, cold ones. And then the plane began shuddering out of control. It was breaking apart." Hugging her arms around herself for warmth she whispered, "I was so useless. While I huddled alone in the darkness, my mother tried to alert a nearby airport.

"My father was an experienced pilot. He was completely professional. But right before we went down, he said, 'We love you, baby. Never forget that.'" Kirsten shuddered. "Then there was only the terrible sound of the crash. One moment there was a deafening roar and then...silence. All around me lay twisted metal and shards of glass. When the searchlights grew closer, I could make out the bodies of my parents. That was when I blacked out."

Hearing the sob in her throat, Stefan looked down into her ashen face. Ignoring the crowd, which was still staring in fascination at the sky, he hauled her inside the control tower.

"Kirsten, that was a long time ago."

Dazed, she continued staring, seeing nothing. She found it impossible to speak.

"Kirsten, I'm sorry. It's the sight of Drew's plane that's made you relive that scene again."

"I shouldn't have come."

"What are you talking about?"

"Don't you see. I didn't want to come. But I knew it was a chance to see you again." Her voice broke. "Andrew isn't going to make it. Just like my father and mother. It's all going wrong."

"Shh." He led her to a chair and gently forced her to sit. Kneeling in front of her, he took her hands in his. They were cold, icy cold. "Drew's an expert pilot. There are always little things that go wrong. He's prepared for them. These aircraft have backup instruments."

"You don't understand, do you? My father was an expert, too. And he had my mother there to help. But nothing could save them." She sobbed, covering her face with her hands. "They were so busy trying to comfort me that they gave their lives."

His voice was low, angry. "Stop this, Kirsten. Do you hear me?"

Yanking her to her feet, he shook her roughly before drawing her into his arms. With his mouth pressed to her hair he swore savagely, then said, "You shouldn't feel guilty because you survived and they died. You survived that plane crash because you were meant to live.''

Her breath caught in her throat. How had he managed to cut through everything and get to the real cause of her pain? "No," she sobbed. "I should have died with them.''

His voice was urgent. "More than anything your parents would have wanted you to live your life to the fullest. I believe that all our destinies are charted at the moment of birth. We can make choices, change courses many times. But we cannot change our destiny. That's in the hands of fate.''

Placing his hand under her chin, he forced her to meet his angry look. "Andrew is not going to die today. He's fated to live a long and productive life." As she tried to turn away he caught her chin and held it firmly. His voice was a low rasp. "Just as you're fated to love me, whether you care to admit it or not.''

A voice over the speaker intoned, "Perfect landing, Fox One. General Russault offers his congratulations on having successfully qualified as a pilot for the F-15s.''

Andrew's calm voice caused her to blink. "That was just about the smoothest landing I've ever made. Thank the general for me. And tell my father to break out the champagne. We're going to celebrate.''

Outside, a cheer went up from the observers. In the control room, the technicians were slapping one another on the back. Smiling, they gave a thumbs-up sign to the prince as he strolled across the airfield. Kirsten's eyes misted as Stefan wrapped his arms around her in a bear hug. Lifting her off her feet, he swung her around, hugged her again, then drew her close and kissed her.

She was still reeling from the kiss when Andrew rushed in and threw his arms around his brother.

"How'd I do, big brother?"

Stefan's voice was gruff. "You did us proud, Drew."

Andrew touched Kirsten's cheek. "Tears? On my special day? I hope they're tears of happiness." Giving a quick glance at Stefan he muttered, "You look a little pale, Kirsten." Swinging her around, he dropped a kiss on her cheek. "You'd better lend her some of your vitality, Stefan. Better yet, bring her out in the sun. And see that she drinks some champagne." Before he could say more, his family rushed forward, deluging him with hugs and kisses. Glasses of champagne were passed around.

Softly, Kirsten whispered, "Stefan, I'm sorry for the hysterics. You deserved better at a time like this. Drew is right. I can't match your strength or the strength of your wonderful family."

He touched a finger to her lips to silence her. "Nonsense. You're the strongest woman I know. And now that you've given me a glimpse of what you went through as a child, I have even more respect for your spirit." He caught her hand and led her toward the others. "Come on. This is Drew's big day. Let's share his happiness with him."

Someone handed Kirsten a glass of champagne. Sipping, she glanced at Andrew, still dressed in his military uniform, his helmet carelessly tossed on a nearby chair. His shirtfront and sides were damp from perspiration. His hair was plastered to his head. He wore the flush of success with casual grace. Around him, his family basked in his glory.

Alana looked up to see her staring. Stepping closer, she asked, "Aren't you glad you came?"

Kirsten swallowed. Glad? The most painful part of her past had been forced into the open. This was the first time she'd ever spoken about the crash. The first time she'd ever admitted aloud the guilt she'd borne all those years. Though she felt drained, she also felt that a crushing burden had been lifted from her.

She smiled. For the first time today, her heart felt light. "I'm very glad, Alana. Thank you."

"What are you thanking my sister for?" Stefan asked as he joined them.

"For bringing me." She looked up to meet his steady gaze. "For making me face an old enemy."

"No enemies in this room. Only friends. We'll be leaving shortly, Alana."

"Oh," she said. "I sent my driver home earlier. We'll go back with Michael."

"Sorry," Stefan interrupted. "You and Michael will be going back with Father."

"And what about Kirsten?"

Stefan took the glass from Kirsten's hand and handed it to an aide. Giving his sister a cool look he said, "I'm borrowing Michael's car to drive Kirsten home."

"But . . ."

"It's all been arranged. We'll see you later."

After proudly clapping Andrew's back and embracing him in a fierce hug, Stefan steered Kirsten out of the control tower. Behind them, his family exchanged knowing smiles.

With his arm around her shoulders, he led her toward a sleek red roadster.

"I'll put the top up, if you'd like," Stefan offered.

She gave him a brilliant smile. "No. I want to feel the sun on my face and the wind in my hair." As she settled herself inside she lifted her arms to the sky. "Suddenly I feel very lighthearted."

"Just don't faint on me," he muttered. Turning, he caught a wisp of her hair and wrapped it around his finger. The color was returning to her cheeks. For a moment in there, he'd worried that her childhood memories were too painful to bear. Now it looked as if she had herself under control once more.

"How about dinner somewhere? Just the two of us."

The seductive tone of his voice brought her back to earth. "No, Stefan. Not tonight."

"You've made other plans?"

She nodded. Tonight she intended to order a simple meal at the villa and be in bed by dark. The emotional battering of the day had taken its toll. She was totally exhausted.

Turning on the ignition, he touched the accelerator, and the little car shot along the smooth highway. Behind them, a dark car followed at a discreet distance.

As they approached the checkpoint, Kirsten caught her breath. "I forgot about Henri Soulier."

"What about him?"

Lifting a hand against the sun's glare, she said, "He was there when Alana and I arrived. The soldiers refused to allow him to go any farther. He asked if he could ride to the airstrip with us, but one of the soldiers checked a list of guests and barred his way."

"Odd." Stefan saluted the soldiers and drove on.

"Alana was very diplomatic. She even offered to ask her father's permission when he arrived. But Soulier said that would be too late."

"Too late." Lighting a cigarette, Stefan squinted and exhaled a stream of smoke. Then, chuckling, he added, "Maybe Henri wanted to go up with Drew."

"He doesn't strike me as a man of courage, but of cunning."

"Cunning." Stefan gave her a quick glance before returning his concentration to the road. "It's plain Henri is unhappy. But I've never thought of him as a clever man."

"Maybe he bears watching."

"Henri Soulier? He and my father are distant cousins." Stefan crushed his cigarette in the ashtray and floored the accelerator. "Hold on. I'm about to give you the ride of your life."

With a little laugh, Kirsten watched the colors of the lush countryside merge and blend into a brilliant kaleidoscope. The air was heavy with the sweet fragrance of millions of flowers. What must it be like to live with such beauty for a lifetime?

With a squeal of tires, the little car stopped outside Kirsten's villa.

Switching off the car, Stefan turned to her. Removing his sunglasses, he allowed his gaze to make a slow journey over her figure. He liked the way her hair looked, still primly pulled back at her nape, with little wind-tossed tendrils kissing her cheeks. Her eyes danced with laughter. The sun and fresh air had brought a soft pink to her cheeks.

Touching a finger to her mouth, he traced the outline of her full lower lip. Her throat went dry. She saw his eyes darken slightly, from gold to glimmering bronze.

"I was determined to avoid you today," he muttered.

"Sorry I spoiled your plans."

"I would have phoned you eventually, anyway. It was inevitable." His finger followed the curve of her cheek. "I wouldn't have been able to stand the thought of not seeing you."

He leaned closer, inhaling the fragrance that was uniquely hers.

Out of the corner of her eye she could see an armed man stepping from the car behind them. She stiffened. "I'd better get in."

"I'll walk you."

Before she could protest, he was out of the car and holding her door. Catching her hand, he walked with her along the front walk of her villa. When she found her key, he took it from her hand and opened the door.

She turned, determined to bar his way. "Thank you, Stefan. I'm happy for Drew."

He grinned. "Since you're too shy to ask, I'll invite myself in." In one swift motion he stepped inside and closed the door firmly.

The coolness of the interior was refreshing after the heat of the sun. Gauzy drapes had been drawn against the light. The villa bore the distinctive scent of her cologne.

"We could order dinner here and spend a cozy evening in your pool."

"No," she protested quickly, then tried to soften her refusal. "I'm really tired."

"Then I'll see that you get to bed early."

His easy smile caused her heart to trip over itself. Outside, she heard muted footsteps as Stefan's men positioned themselves around the villa.

Her smile fled. "I need to be alone tonight."

"Kirsten..."

She evaded his touch and walked into the bedroom. Tossing her purse onto the bed, she slipped off her navy jacket and placed it on a hanger in the closet.

Stefan stood in the doorway watching her. Here her fragrance was even stronger, mixed with the exotic scent of lavender soap.

His gaze was arrested by the limp gown hanging over the door of the closet.

"I almost forgot. I'll take that with me."

"Let me have it cleaned first."

"No." Moving closer, he lifted it down and draped it over his arm. At her arched eyebrow he explained, "This is such a simple thing. Besides, it gives me pleasure to do something for you."

She walked him to the door, grateful for his quiet acceptance of her decision to spend the evening alone. "What will you do tonight?"

He turned. Sunlight filtered through the glass panels on either side of the door, giving her a soft, ethereal appearance. She was a vision of light and beauty.

With one arm he drew her close. "I'll dine with my family. We'll celebrate Drew's successful flight. And when night covers the land, and we go our separate ways, I'll stand by my window and think of you." His lips roamed her temple, her cheek, lighting a fire deep inside her. "And if you've any heart at all, you'll stir in your sleep and wish I were here beside you."

She moved her face, loving the feel of his lips on her skin. At her movement, he drew her closer and kissed the tip of her nose.

Her eyes widened, meeting his amber gaze. She was drowning in those golden depths. "Kiss me, Kirsten."

He wasn't smiling. The look on his face was so intense it frightened her.

"Kiss me. Let me feel you, warm and willing, the way I've wanted all day to feel you."

She couldn't help herself. Wrapping her arms around his waist, she drew herself closer to him, then closer still, until she could feel his entire length against her. Bringing her lips to his, she moved them ever so gently against his. Instantly the flame of passion flickered to life. She stopped, stunned by the jolt she felt at that simple touch. Catching her breath, she glanced up at his face. He showed absolutely no emotion.

She'd imagined it. She brought her lips to his once more. They touched lightly. And then touched again. The gown he was holding slipped from his arm and fell to the floor at their feet. His arms pinned her, holding her firmly against him. His mouth opened, inviting her to taste him. She brought her arms up around his neck, drawing his head even closer. She couldn't get enough of his rich, dark flavor.

She spoke his name and moaned softly as she clung to him, offering her lips. He took and drank deeply and took more until she felt drained. And still he continued to kiss her until she was no longer capable of conscious thought.

"Let me stay."

It was what she wanted. What they both wanted.

Drawing away, she took in great gulps of air and fought to clear her head.

"I want you to go now."

He stared at her heaving breasts and marveled at her fierce determination.

"If that's what you really want."

She ran a tongue over her lips and tasted him. It wasn't at all what she wanted. But one of them had to be sensible.

"Good night, Stefan." Holding the door, she watched as he bent and lifted the wilted gown from the floor.

Brushing past her, he stalked to the car. He dropped the gown on the passenger seat and settled himself inside. Pulling a cigarette from his gold case, he held a flame to the tip. His hand was trembling.

Chapter Eleven

The muffled sound of a phone disturbed Kirsten's deep slumber. For long moments she couldn't figure out what the sound was. Then, rolling to her side, she removed the pillow from the telephone.

Last night room service had sent her the wrong dinner. After a second call, they'd corrected their mistake. Later, just as she was dozing, the front desk had called to apologize. That was when Kirsten had taken drastic measures to ensure that she would sleep undisturbed.

Lifting the receiver, she mumbled a greeting.

"Kirsten?" Stefan's voice sounded wary.

"Good morning." She felt suddenly tongue-tied.

The sound of her husky voice made Stefan ache with need. "I have an appointment to visit the hospital on a goodwill mission this afternoon. Will you come with me?"

She would have accepted any excuse to be with him for another day. And luckily this would be a public appearance; Stefan would have no opportunity to repeat the last night's awkward scene. She deliberately kept her tone light. "I suppose. Yes, I'd like that."

"Good. I'll pick you up around noon. That way we can have lunch first."

"Would you like me to order something here in my villa? It's no trouble."

She heard the smile in his voice. "I wish we could. I'd prefer to be alone with you. But we're invited to eat in the hospital cafeteria with the staff."

"That should provide enough chaperones to keep you from getting fresh with me."

"Want to bet? You know how I love a dare. I'll see you at noon."

She leaned her head back, recalling the thrill she felt each time Stefan touched her. He would be an attentive lover. Instantly she dismissed the tempting thought from her mind and replaced it with a more sobering one; he was a prince.

Tossing aside the bed linens, Kirsten hastily pulled on a bikini. A vigorous swim would release any lingering tensions.

As she stepped out on the patio she lifted her face to the sun. It was going to be another glorious day.

She knew the moment he crossed the patio and entered her room. It had become a game between them.

Keeping her back to the door, she said, "I feel a chill. Must have left that door open again. No telling what kind of creature might find its way inside."

"Maybe a rabid dog," he whispered, coming up behind her.

"Umm, more like a wolf," she murmured, arching her neck as he nuzzled her shoulder.

"Nice of you to wear something so...obliging." Running his finger under the narrow strap of her sundress, he slid it down her arm and pressed his mouth against her satin skin. "I can see who's going to be the center of attention at the hospital."

"I have a very proper jacket that goes over this," she said, pulling up the strap and taking a step away from him.

Strong hands caught her, firmly turning her around. His gaze swept the pale blue camisole and narrow white skirt that accentuated her trim figure. "That's a shame. I like looking at your bare shoulders. Do you have freckles anywhere else besides here?" Without warning he bent his lips to a line of freckles that paraded across her upper arm.

"I'm never going to tell you." Kirsten found that she had to fight to keep her voice steady.

"You won't have to. I intend to see for myself." Reaching into his breast pocket, he said without preamble, "I brought you something."

"Stefan, not again."

He saw her gaze shift to his pocket in anticipation. "Well, maybe I have been overdoing it." He shrugged. "Never mind."

"You mean you'd keep it from me just because I made a little protest?"

He fought to keep the laughter from his voice. "I wouldn't want to spoil you."

Grinning, she reached a hand toward his pocket. "Go ahead. Spoil me."

He allowed her to slip her hand inside. When she felt the envelope, she glanced up. He was watching her with a sly smile.

"You're allowed to look inside."

Tearing open the envelope, she gave a little sound of pleasure. It was a photograph of the two of them dancing. She hadn't even noticed a photographer in attendance at the party. But then, everything at the palace was done discreetly. In the picture, she was enfolded in Stefan's arms. He was staring down at her with an expression of adoration. Her head was tilted upward; she was gazing raptly at him. Their lips hovered mere inches apart. It would have been apparent to anyone watching them that they were completely absorbed in each other.

She glanced up, then away, feeling heat stain her cheeks. He was watching her too closely.

"Thank you."

"You're welcome. Since you insist on keeping us apart, I thought you might want this reminder of how perfectly we fit together."

"It'll make a great souvenir," she said, turning away. It was getting harder to keep up this teasing banter. "I'll get my jacket."

As she hurried to her bedroom, Stefan frowned. His need for her was becoming nearly impossible to ignore.

"And this is the pediatric wing, Your Highness."

The doctor, crisp in his white lab coat, respectfully stood aside to allow the prince and his guest to step out of the elevator first. Opening double doors, he led the way down a spotless hallway.

In the cheerful ward, the walls were painted with colorful characters from nursery rhymes. Each hospital bed had a quilt printed with matching characters. At their arrival, nurses and technicians in starched uniforms looked up from their duties with expectant smiles. But it wasn't the cozy decor or the efficiency and cleanliness that Kirsten noted. It was the children.

Stopping at the first bed, she took the hand of a fragile-looking girl whose pale face was the only thing visible beneath her bulky bandages.

"Looks like you've had a nasty accident."

The girl nodded shyly.

"Auto accident," the nurse whispered. "The rest of her family didn't survive. Ever since she learned the truth, she's refused to eat."

Instantly Kirsten knelt and smoothed the girl's damp cheek. In a voice she knew the other children could hear, she said cheerfully, "Look who's come to visit you. Prince Stefan."

Children's heads turned. In this small country, Kirsten knew, even its youngest citizens were aware of the importance of the royal family. The little girl turned to stare at the handsome young man who stood at the front of her bed.

"The prince?"

Kirsten nodded and stood aside as Stefan knelt at the girl's side.

"I hope you're going to be out of here soon," he murmured, bending to kiss her bandaged cheek.

"I have nowhere to go." A tear squeezed its way from the little girl's eye.

"I have a lovely house in the country," Stefan said, stroking her head. "With horses and ponies, and two of the loneliest cats you've ever seen. They'd love to entertain some children." Glancing at Kirsten, he added, "My brothers and I thought we'd give a little party for some of the children here when you're well enough. Would you like that?"

A tiny smile touched her lips. "Oh, yes."

"Good." He lifted her hand to his mouth, then gently tucked it beneath the blankets. "What's your name?"

"Cory," the little girl said with some importance. She knew the others in the room were watching and listening.

"Cory, I'll let the doctors tell me when you're strong enough to come to my party."

As he walked to the next bed, the little girl watched him with adoring eyes.

Deliberately keeping her tone soft, Kirsten asked, "Do you have any aunts or uncles, Cory?"

"I have an aunt Betty. I've never met her. She lives in America."

"Maybe when you're well enough, you can go to live with your Aunt Betty."

The girl turned her head away. "I'm afraid to go there."

"Why?"

Wide green eyes lifted to meet Kirsten's. "There're cowboys and Indians there. And all kinds of wild animals."

Smiling widely, Kirsten asked, "Now who filled your head with those stories?"

"Aaren." The girl pointed to a boy of about six, whose arm was in a cast.

"Well, I live in America, and I've never seen a cowboy except in the movies. One of my friends married a man from an Indian tribe in Arizona, and I've heard she's very happy. And as for wild animals, the wildest one I've ever seen is a neighbor's dog, Aarfie, who likes to chew children's mittens."

The children around her shrieked with laughter.

By this time, Stefan and the doctor were pausing to watch as she continued to enchant the children with stories of her hometown. Before long, she had picked up a book about two bears who wanted to move from their cave to an apartment in the city. Changing her voice to impersonate first the gruff father bear and then the sweet mother bear, she began to weave a magic tale.

A little boy crawled up on Kirsten's lap and reached out to touch her hair. A second child, his head bandaged, settled down beside her. Without missing a word, she placed an arm around his waist, allowing the boy to turn the pages of the book. When the story ended, a chorus of children's voices begged for more. Glancing up, Kirsten lifted an eyebrow at Stefan.

"We'll go on to the next ward, then come back for you." She smiled gratefully, picked up a second book and began to read.

Stefan paused in the doorway and watched Kirsten with the children. She had moved to a bed in the center of the room. All the children were clustered around her, some on her lap or beside her on the bed, others on mats on the floor. Those who were confined to their beds had been positioned nearby so that they could hear her voice clearly. Every child's attention was focused on her as she read.

The little boy on her lap was resting his head on her shoulder. One chubby hand was twined in her hair. A little girl beside her was tucked firmly beneath her arm. Kirsten's hair drifted forward, framing her face. Reading the villain's part, she made her voice appropriately fierce. The children roared. When she read the happy ending, the children cheered and clapped. Even the nurses, Stefan noted, had paused in their work to enjoy her performance.

She was so natural with children. In their company there was no trace of shyness. With these lonely, frightened children, she was free to reach out and simply love.

Love. He felt giddy suddenly. He loved this woman. In her he saw a goodness, a sweetness that he had been searching for all his life. He wanted her to love him back. He wanted her to share his life. He wanted her to bear his children. The thought left him stunned.

Kirsten glanced up. Seeing the strange look on Stefan's face, she forgot what she was reading. When he saw that she was watching he composed himself and walked toward her with a bland smile. She blinked. Had she just imagined that look?

"The doctor tells me his young patients need a nap before dinner."

The children groaned in unison.

With a laugh, Kirsten stood, still holding the little boy who had been on her lap. Though he, too, protested, she knew he was nearly asleep in her arms.

"The doctor knows what's good for you. If you want to get well soon, you must follow his orders."

"Will you bring Miss Stevens back soon?" one of the children called.

Stefan smiled. "I'd like to persuade Miss Stevens to become a regular visitor here."

Giving him a quick look, she tucked the little boy into his bed, then walked to Cory's side. Kneeling down, she whispered, "I don't know if I'll get a chance to see you again before I leave, but I'd like the doctor to give me your aunt's address in America."

"Will you come see me?" the little girl asked.

"If I can."

"Have you ever been scared?" The plaintive voice quivered at the question.

Staring down into those sad, frightened eyes, Kirsten swallowed. "I know exactly how you feel. I lost my parents in an accident, Cory. When I was forced to leave the city to live with my grandmother on a farm, I thought I'd die from the loneliness. But I learned to love her very much. And she taught me more than she ever knew." Kissing the girl's cheek, she added, "Your wounds will heal. And so will your heart. But it takes time. Let the people who love you help."

The little girl forced a brave smile. "I love you, Miss Stevens." Glancing beyond her, she added, "Thank you, Prince Stefan, for bringing her here today."

With a last wave at the children, Kirsten allowed herself to be led from the ward. As they rode the elevator, both she and Stefan were lost in quiet contemplation.

The king sat silently in his study, listening to a report on his son's hospital visit. According to his aide, the prince's companion, Miss Stevens, had charmed the patients and staff. At the staff luncheon, she had asked intelligent questions, and had been especially interested in the newly acquired equipment. In the wards, she had been concerned and compassionate without being intrusive. But it was in the children's ward that she had blossomed.

The king dismissed his aide, then allowed himself to smile for the first time. His thoughts were on his wife. It was her beauty that had initially attracted him. But it was her kindness, her dedication to his people, that had won his heart.

It was obvious from this young woman's choice of career, and from her actions at the hospital, that she was a concerned, caring person. Her behavior confirmed what the king had read earlier. The investigation he had launched after he'd first learned of his son's interest in this stranger had produced some fascinating information. The king thumbed through the neatly typed pages of the report. Kirsten's father had been a pilot and war hero. The authorities investigating the accident that had claimed his life and his wife's indicated that he had taken heroic measures to avoid injuring anyone on the ground. From the investiga-

tor's report, Kirsten's paternal grandmother had
helped mold Kirsten into the independent, spirited
person she'd become. This multifaceted young woman
sounded like the perfect mate for the future king of
Maurab. Now, the king thought, turning to study the
surf crashing onto the rocks below, he had to find a
way to convince those two young people of that fact.

It wasn't possible, Kirsten thought, for time to pass
so quickly. She had toured the countryside, and had
fallen in love with Stefan's rural estate. Set on twenty
acres of wooded, rolling hills, it reminded her of a
sprawling French cottage, with brick-paved court-
yards and stables for a dozen horses. Comfortable
plaid and chintz upholstered furniture set around huge
open fireplaces added to the relaxed atmosphere. Most
of the staff had been with Stefan since he was a boy.
There in that country setting, surrounded by the things
of his youth, Kirsten could imagine what he'd been
like as a child. She knew family was important to him.
Like King Alaric, he would be a loving but firm father. She found herself wondering which member of
Europe's elite would share Stefan's love of children.
The thought was too painful to dwell on.

Kirsten dressed carefully. This was to be her first
dinner in Stefan's private apartment at the palace. The
only other time she'd been there, she hadn't even noticed her surroundings.

Her dress was of rich, sapphire blue silk with a
graceful, draped neckline that dipped to her waist in
back. Because it was backless, she wore nothing beneath. She had found this dress in a little boutique at
the hotel. The eager young salesgirl had assured her it
was prefectly proper, but now studying her reflection

in a full-length mirror, Kirsten began to have doubts about her choice. Something more demure would be safer, she decided. She began rummaging through her closet for a replacement.

A knock on her front door ended her search. There wasn't time to change. Giving herself a last glance in the mirror, she caught up her bag and hurried to the door.

"I expected you to come in through the terrace," she said by way of greeting.

"I've never cared much for doing the expected." Stefan's gaze slowly swept over her, lingering a moment on her flushed cheeks, then moving meaningfully to her bare shoulders. "Love those freckles." He grinned as her flush deepened. "In fact, the whole view is enjoyable."

"You say things like that just to make me uncomfortable," she said, nudging him out the door.

"You're beginning to figure me out." He paused and brushed his lips over her temple. "I can't resist teasing you. That blush on your cheeks is so becoming."

"I wonder if you're going to think the lump on your head is as attractive."

"Remember my bodyguards." He ducked as she playfully swung her hand, then caught it and brought it to his lips. "Come on. Let's get in the car before LeClerc dashes out here to investigate what you're doing to me."

As he began to drive, Stefan said nonchalantly, "There's something for you in back."

"What?"

"See for yourself."

Kneeling on the seat, she turned on the overhead light and reached for the handles of an enormous shopping bag. Setting it between them, she lifted out a fuzzy stuffed animal with shaggy fur and the saddest eyes she'd ever seen.

Hugging it to her, she laughed. "He's wonderful."

"He's ugly," Stefan returned.

"Well, yes, but he's so ugly he's cute. What is he?"

"You don't know? He's a buffalo. I thought all Americans knew their buffalo."

At her puzzled expression, he added, "Cory thought America was filled with cowboys and Indians. I thought a buffalo would be appropriate. You know. Give me a home, where the buffalo roam . . ."

"With your logic, it figures." Her eyes crinkled as she laughed. Studying the creature, she said solemnly, "He needs a name. Something typically American." With a sudden gleam in her eye, she declared, "Bill."

"Bill? That's typically American?"

"You've never heard of Buffalo Bill?"

Stefan laughed heartily. He was relaxed, euphoric and in love with the most beautiful, the most wonderful, the craziest woman in the world. And tonight, by God, he was going to convince her that she was in love with him, as well.

As the driver behind them fought to keep up, the little sports car shot through the gathering shadows of evening. A few minutes later it stopped with a squeal of tires outside the palace door.

Chapter Twelve

Despite the fact that she had been in it once before, Kirsten wasn't at all prepared for Stefan's private apartment. On that other occasion, she had formed only the most hazy impression of it.

Now, crossing a brick-paved courtyard, she paused to watch the water from an intricately carved stone fountain play softly against the tiny winking lights of the garden. Beyond, a pond shimmered in the light of the moon. Gently circling the glassy surface of the water was a pair of graceful swans.

In the darkness, he saw her eyes shimmering with pleasure. "Oh, Stefan, this is lovely."

"Humble, but home," he quipped. Then his tone warmed. "It's my retreat."

Catching her hand, Stefan circled the main portion of the building and entered through a private door.

From the moment she stepped across the threshold, she felt as if she'd entered another world. Their footsteps were muffled by thick, white carpeting. Enormous pottery vases held masses of flowers and vines, filling the room with lush fragrance.

As soon as the door closed behind them, a big dog lumbered toward them, pressing his nose into Stefan's palm.

"Bruno. Good boy. Give the lady one of your best-behaved welcomes."

Beside him, Kirsten knelt and ran a hand over the thick, shiny coat. In response, the dog gave her a wet kiss.

"Is this the same menacing monster I first encountered on the beach?" she asked with a laugh.

"The same. Bruno can be as gentle as a lamb with those he loves. All the same, he's trained to attack on command."

When she heard his words, Kirsten's hand paused in its movement. Glancing up at Stefan's serious look, she realized he wasn't teasing.

"You keep an attack dog as a pet?"

"All our dogs are trained to protect us. Still, they're loyal, loving animals. Bruno's been with me for five years. He considers himself one of the family."

Having received his measure of affection, the dog walked to a corner of the room and curled himself into a circle. Though he appeared relaxed, his intelligent brown eyes watched his master's every movement.

Two steps down from the entrance foyer they entered a library-sitting room, with comfortable leather sofas and high-backed tweed chairs. The walls were lined with bookshelves. A quick glance at the titles showed their owner had an inquiring, imaginative mind.

Picking up a book, Kirsten quoted the opening line without even opening it.

"More proof that we have the same tastes," Stefan remarked. "Did you come to borrow my books, or to eat my food?"

She gave a quick laugh. "Maybe both."

Walking up behind her, he took the book from her hand. "Maybe I have other things in mind." At her wide-eyed look, he added softly, "We have too much in common to consider our meeting simply an accident." His warm breath feathered the hair at her temple, stirring something deep inside her. His voice sent tremors along her spine. "It was fate."

She refused to look at him. "We're as different as two people can be. I belong in Fairfield, Ohio. You're at home all over the world. The salary I earn wouldn't pay your telephone bill. I live by schedules, and you said you hate regimentation."

Turning her in his arms, he whispered, "Minor differences. We're entitled to a few. Besides," he countered, running a finger down her nose, "those are the things that spice up a relationship."

"We don't have a relationship, Stefan."

He caught her chin, forcing her to meet his steady look. "We should have. Why do you insist on denying what your heart already knows?"

Jerking her face away, she took a step backward, and was stopped by the bookshelf. She knew what he wanted of her. She also knew it would make their inevitable parting even more painful.

"Are you going to feed me, or are we going to waste the night arguing?"

He smiled indulgently and caught her hand. Patience. He was gradually learning he had more than he'd known. "Come. Tour the rest of my apartment while I see to the last details."

Beyond the library was a magnificent living room done in white and caramel. The sofas and chairs were stylish art deco, with a three-tiered coffee table. Above, a skylight opened the room to the night sky.

To the left of this room were the master bedroom and bath. The door to the bedroom stood open, piquing her interest. A massive king-size bed of solid brass dominated the room. Caramel-colored sheets and pillows were visible beneath an ornately embroidered satin and velvet quilt of gold and silver. Beside the bed was a Louis XIV writing table, its entire top covered with family photographs. The silver frame closest to the bed held the caricature of Stefan that she'd drawn.

Across the room, two love seats in caramel-and-white plaid were pulled up in front of a marble fireplace. Regally ensconced in one of the sofas was a huge white ball of fur. Tentatively, Kirsten stepped closer to investigate.

From her vantage point in the middle of the room, Kirsten could make out a huge sunken tub of bronze-veined marble, just beyond a half-open door. Pots of vines and flowers could be seen in one corner of the bathroom.

"Dinner is almost ready," Stefan announced, appearing behind her and handing her a tulip glass of white wine.

"Thank you." She felt his gaze on her as she sipped.

"Feel free to look around."

Kirsten hesitated, but she couldn't contain her curiosity.

"I was just curious about your cat."

"The Countess?"

Kirsten laughed. "Is that her name, or her royal title?"

"Both. She's a mean old cat who was given to me when I was only eleven. Her equally ornery offspring have been sent into exile at my country place. But The Countess has earned the right to live out her life here."

As he spoke, Stefan led Kirsten toward the fireplace. The sleepy cat looked up, then stretched and yawned.

As Kirsten scratched her ears, he warned, "Watch her claws. The Countess likes to test my guests' threshold of pain."

"How can he call you mean?" Kirsten murmured, as the old cat rolled over to allow her belly to be rubbed. "You're just a sweet old kitty."

"That sweet old kitty puts Bruno in his place whenever he gets too playful."

"Good girl. Always keep the upper hand." Kirsten laughed, and the cat purred.

Stefan shook his head. "I don't know what magic power you have. I think you're the first person ever to escape the slash of those claws."

"She knows a friend when she sees one. Besides, I'm the best back-scratcher in Fairfield."

"I'll have to remember that."

Choosing to ignore his teasing tone, Kirsten glanced toward the desk top. "I'm curious to see your photographs." She indicated the cluttered pictures. "I want to see how you looked as a boy."

Leading the way, he paused to watch her as she bent to examine each photo.

"Your hair was so much lighter. You were practically a blonde."

He was amused at her surprise. Photographs of him had been made public from the time he was born. "It didn't last long. By the time I started school, my hair was as dark as my father's. I remember worrying that my hair wouldn't be like his. When I was very young, I thought I had to be everything, do everything the king did."

"When did you decide to become a rebel?"

He laughed at her choice of words. "I suppose it was when I realized that I could never live quite like other boys. Rebellion can take many forms."

She nodded, recalling her own unexplained immobility after the accident.

"And now? Are you still rebelling?" she asked, picking up a small framed portrait of his parents as bride and groom.

"Maybe this—" he waved a hand at his surroundings "—is a form of rebellion. I've always insisted on my privacy. My attitude paved the way for the rest of the family to secure their own apartments within the palace walls. And of course, there were the frequent escapes." At her questioning look, he added, "Always, I've had a strong need to slip away from the rigid confines of this country, this life-style."

He sipped his wine, enjoying the way her hair looked in the lamplight. "But in the past two weeks, I've felt a change, a willingness to conform that I've never known before." He chuckled. "My sudden contentment has my father confounded."

Choosing to ignore the implication of his words, she studied the look of adoration on the faces of the two people in the photograph. "Your parents seem so young in this picture."

"They were. I suppose there's no timetable when it comes to falling in love. My mother was only twenty, my father barely twenty-one when they were married. By comparison, I'm over the hill." He held out his hand. "Come. We'll eat now."

With a last glance at the smiling pictures of his family, Kirsten followed him.

A table for two had been set on a small terrace in a tiny formal garden. From here, they could hear the pounding of the surf far below. Out on the ocean, lights from passing ships cast a silvery glow.

Two members of the staff saw to their every need, from keeping their wineglasses filled to serving the various dishes. Just beyond the lights of the terrace, Kirsten could make out the silhouettes of the guards, moving silently in the shadows. Stefan seemed completely unaware of their presence. He had eyes only for her.

While Kirsten nibbled a wonderful salad of artichoke hearts in a light vinaigrette dressing, Stefan told her about his experiences at sea.

"Why did you choose the navy?" she asked.

"I've always loved the sea and ships. Each member of the royal family must choose a branch of the armed services."

While he spoke, a maid removed their salad plates and served the main course, delicate slivers of veal on a bed of wild rice. With barely a pause, Stefan continued. "Alex loved heavy equipment. Tanks. Andrew loves planes. He's been a flying buff since he was a kid."

"And Michael?"

Stefan smiled, thinking about his youngest brother. "Computers, I suspect. He has a quick mind and loves anything electronic. Plus, he's the sharpest chess player I've ever met. My guess is he'll lead our country into the computer age of warfare."

"Why must you think of war?"

Seeing her frown, he covered her hand with his. Feeling the sudden jerk of her pulse, he smiled gently. "Though we don't like to think of it, there is evil in the world. Only a fool would hide his head in the sand. We must be prepared for any eventuality. Especially in our position. My father is chief of the country's armed forces, but even more important, he is a peacekeeper."

"Aren't those two opposed—the head of the armed forces and a peacekeeper?"

He sipped the wine. "He mediates between the country's rival political factions. I've seen him brave shouting hecklers and angry mobs of protesters. My father has raised all of us to defend democracy with our lives."

Kirsten felt admiration for the man who seemed to rule his country with sheer charisma. "I've heard that the king unites without dominating."

Stefan nodded. "My father has more real power than any other European monarch. Yet he remains a modest family man."

Kirsten realized that this man who would be king had an extraordinary example to follow. It was hard to imagine there were some who would wish him harm. The thought caused her to tremble.

Feeling her tremor, he brought her to her feet and wrapped an arm about her shoulders. "The breeze off the water is cool. We'll take our dessert by the fire."

It wasn't the breeze, Kirsten knew. It was his words that had created the sudden chill. It was terrible to think about living with such fears. She could never handle his world. It was too alien to her.

Discreetly, a maid carried a silver coffee service to the bronze table that had been drawn up before the fire in the bedroom. While she poured coffee, a second maid transferred marzipan and glazed fruit from a silver tray to two crystal plates. After adding a decanter of brandy and two snifters, both maids left quietly.

Bruno settled himself comfortably before the fire. From her spot on the sofa, The Countess purred her contentment.

While Stefan warmed the brandy, he watched Kirsten slip off her shoes and tuck her feet beneath her on the sofa.

"Room for dessert?"

"If I eat any more, I'll burst."

Holding a sugar-coated strawberry to her lips, he murmured, "You forget. I've learned some of your weaknesses."

Opening her mouth, she accepted the fruit and sighed. "I'd better watch out. I don't want to let you in on all my secrets."

"I know too many already," he murmured, brushing his lips lightly over hers. She tasted of strawberry and sweet sugar glaze. "You're a pushover for children and animals. You'll accept my gifts, as long as they're not expensive." When she started to protest, he held a second strawberry to her mouth and swallowed back a laugh as she tried, and failed, to refuse it. "And although you try to act cool to the idea, you're not as repulsed by the thought of our making love as you suggest."

She nearly choked on the strawberry. Repulsed? Nothing could be further from the truth.

"You have an ego problem, Stefan. And as for dessert, that's the last time I'm going to give in." She squelched the impulse to reach for another berry.

"I hope not," he muttered, tracing a finger along the outline of her lips.

Butterflies invaded her stomach. "Don't."

"Don't what?" He caught a stray strand of her hair, enjoying the flush that stole over her cheeks.

"Don't touch me. Don't kiss me. Not here. Not in your bedroom."

His eyes narrowed. She was reminded of cats' eyes. "You ask too much of me."

"And you ask too much of me." Keeping her hand against his chest, she held him away. "It would be so easy to get drawn in to all this—the wealth, the glamour, the sophistication."

"And you resent all this? Are you angry with me because I'm wealthy and pampered, Kirsten?"

She flushed. "Not angry." Her voice lowered. "Maybe I'm just afraid it's all too seductive. When this vacation is over, when I have to go back to my own world, I want to be able to deal with it."

At the vehemance of her words, he said nothing.

"My vacation ends in two days." She stiffened. Two days. The words echoed in her mind. Until this very moment, she hadn't allowed herself to think about it, to mark the time. Where had the days, the hours, gone?

Abruptly she stood and walked to the window. Stefan followed, cautioning himself not to touch her.

The moon was so full and bright that it looked like a stage prop from her school's Halloween play. Far out to sea, the waves trailed ribbons of gold.

"Stay with me, Kirsten." Stefan's voice was husky with emotion.

Two days. Two nights. And an eternity of missing him. "I can't."

Behind her, he drew her roughly against the length of him. As he pressed his lips to her temple, she felt his hands, firm and strong, gripping her shoulders. She needed only to lean back against him, to absorb his strength, and she would know how right it could be.

Lifting her hair, he brought his mouth to her shoulder. She trembled and arched herself, allowing him easier access.

"Your skin tastes so clean, like rainwater," he breathed as he felt her first trembling response. "And here," he murmured, turning her in his arms and bringing his lips to her throat, "your perfume is stronger here. I can taste it, breathe it."

Did he know the power he had over her? She felt her legs buckling and gripped his upper arms for support. Using only his lips, he could make her too weak to stand.

"I want to go now."

For the length of a single heartbeat, he hesitated. Then, drawing her closer, he ran his tongue along her throat to her ear. "And I want you to stay," he whispered.

"You're very good at giving orders. I'm sure that's something a prince learns at an early age. And I suppose your air of command was reaffirmed in the military. But I've never been in the navy. And I'm not one of your subjects. I don't have to take orders from you."

He lifted his head and stared down into blue eyes the color of a stormy ocean. "I don't understand your rejection of me or my military training. Your own father was a war hero."

For a moment she stared blankly at him. Then the full meaning of his words struck her. Her eyes narrowed in fury. "How could you possibly know that? I never told you."

His fingers played with a lock of her hair. He stared at it as if fascinated, avoiding her eyes. "My father had you investigated."

"Inves—" She clamped her mouth shut and pushed herself firmly from his arms.

"Kirsten, listen to me."

She stormed to the fireplace and stared at the dying flames. As he began to speak, she started pacing. She didn't want to hear his explanation. She wanted to block out his words. But though she paced, she listened in silence.

"I know you find it insulting. So did I." He didn't bother to tell her of the angry scene between father and son. Stefan had been furious when his father told him of the investigation. "But the king of Maurab has no choice but to investigate anyone who becomes . . . associated with the royal family. He owes it to his country."

"To say nothing of his own curiosity."

"That, too." Stefan took a step closer, but allowed her some distance. "My father was pleased with the report. So pleased, he couldn't wait to tell me. He considers you . . . suitable."

"Suitable." She clenched her hands. "Suitable for what?" She turned bleak eyes to him. "For a tumble in his son's bed?"

"You don't mean that."

She stiffened, looking every inch the school-teacher. "I find your attitude offensive. And as for this—" she swept her hand in a gesture that indicated his apartment "—I can't take any more of this . . . this public exposure."

"I see. You'd rather expose yourself in private."

"That isn't . . . I didn't . . ." She found herself huffing and stopped, seeing for the first time that he was laughing at her.

Her tone was pure ice. "I want to leave, Stefan."

"And I thought I'd made everything so cozy." Giving a last glance at the cat and dog lazing by the fire, he shrugged. "You're right. I'm very good at giving orders. To my staff. To my men in the service. To the people of my country. But a skinny little slip of a girl . . ."

"Skinny. Be careful, Stefan. You're going too far."

He sighed. "All right, Kirsten. I just keep making things worse. We'll play by your rules. I'll take you home."

She was surprised at how easily he'd been persuaded. It wasn't like him. Still, she thought, he was being agreeable. In fact, he had been all night. Relieved, she gave one last glimpse around his beautiful apartment. It was truly cozy. These rooms were surprisingly homey. They reflected Stefan's personality. She could be comfortable here, except that she would never know when a servant might enter, or if a body-guard was lurking just outside the window, or whether the man she loved would be attacked verbally or physically.

The man she loved. The phrase left her stunned. She glanced at his handsome, aristocratic profile. Did she love him? Or was she simply overwhelmed by his wealth and title? How could she possibly love a man who had just admitted that his father had had her background investigated? The angry thoughts slipped away as quickly as they had come. There was no longer any way to deny it. She loved him. And in a matter of days, she would never see him again.

The drive back to the villa was made in strained silence. The thoughts that crowded Kirsten's mind left her at a loss for words.

As she stepped from the car, Stefan's cool voice stopped her. "You forgot Buffalo Bill."

She reached into the back seat and lifted the sad-eyed animal.

When Stefan accompanied her to the door, she turned to say good-night. Instead, he unlocked the door and caught her hand, pulling her inside. Closing the door behind him, he leaned against it.

His voice was rough with frustration. "I want you, Kirsten. From the first moment I saw you, I've thought of nothing but you."

Her throat was dry. Without realizing it, she clutched the buffalo tightly to her chest. Her voice was barely a whisper. "I won't deny that I want you, too."

He seemed too stunned to speak. As a smile spread across his features, she touched his lips to silence him. "But I've never learned how to give my love lightly. And I can't bear this public life of yours. I hate the fact that your bodyguards are just outside the door, sharing the knowledge that you're here with me."

Catching her hand, he kissed the palm, sending tiny spasms along her spine. "Is that the only thing keeping us apart?"

Too dazed at her own boldness to speak, she simply nodded.

Throwing open the door, Stefan called, "LeClerc. I'd like to see you."

Instantly a shadow moved from the darkness to fill the doorway. Now Kirsten was able to see closeup the man who had always been viewed from a distance.

In his hand was an automatic weapon. His shoulders were nearly as wide as the doorway. He seemed to have no neck. His hair was dark, cut very short; his forehead was wide. He might have been handsome in his youth, with dark, expressive eyes and wide sensual lips. His nose was flat, as if it had been broken. He stood with legs apart, looking completely at ease, but Kirsten was certain he was as tightly coiled as a spring. His gaze slid over her with disinterest, then locked on Stefan's.

"I want you and the others to leave."

The man's eyes blinked once. That was the only sign that he'd heard.

"I'll phone you in the morning."

"But..."

"You heard me. I want you to leave now."

The man hesitated, gave one last frigid glance at Kirsten, then nodded and turned away.

When he was gone, Kirsten stared at the closed door, expecting it to open once more.

"Does that set your mind at ease?"

"He's really gone? They've all gone?"

In the silence, her eyes widened. "Are we really alone?"

He nodded.

She swallowed, finding her throat too tight to speak. Finally she whispered, "You'd do that for me?"

"I want whatever makes you happy, Kirsten. When are you going to believe that?"

"I do." She took a step closer and touched his cheek. "I do."

He stood very still, warning himself not to move. He wanted her so badly that he was afraid he'd frighten her. He had to allow her to set the pace.

"And now?" He watched her, keeping his hands firmly at his sides.

Tossing the stuffed animal on a chair, she lifted herself on tiptoe to touch her lips to Stefan's. Against his mouth she breathed, "You're here. I'm here. We're alone. Completely alone."

He felt a shock of desire and absorbed it, fighting for control.

Sliding her hands along his arms, she gripped his shoulders and drew herself firmly against him. "I'm going to hate myself in the morning," she murmured, bringing her lips to his throat.

"Why?"

"Because this is some kind of crazy, beautiful dream. And in the morning I'm going to have to face reality." Moving her mouth against his throat, she felt his sudden intake of breath.

His control was wavering. Catching her hands in his, he lifted them to his lips, gently kissing one palm, then the other. As she watched him, her smile faded.

Slowly, deliberately, he kissed her wrist and the inside of her arm, then dropped light kisses on the sensitive skin of her upper arm until he felt her tremble.

"Do you know what you're doing to me?"

He gave her a triumphant smile. "It's my intention to make you want me." His voice lowered. "As desperately as I've wanted you since I first saw you on that moon-washed beach."

If only it were that simple, Kirsten thought. If only she could want him, without the emotional attachments. But it was no longer simple. She loved. Achingly. Almost painfully. And when this night ended, he would own her heart. When she left Maurab, as she knew she must, she would be leaving a part of herself here with him.

"Oh, Stefan. Hold me. Love me." She wouldn't think about tomorrow. They would hold on to tonight.

Lifting her chin, he stared at her lovely face, as if memorizing every line and curve. With his thumbs he followed the soft arch of her eyebrows, then caressed her high, firm cheekbones. So soft. Her skin was flawless. His thumbs touched her lips, feeling them part for him. His eyes narrowed. She was so incredibly lovely that she took his breath away.

Lowering his head, he brushed her lips with his. Their breath mingled as she slowly released the sigh that had been building inside her.

"Love me, Stefan. Make love with me."

For a moment longer he paused, loving the way she looked, seeing the naked desire in her eyes. Then his mouth covered hers in a searing kiss and he felt passion skyrocket through him, shattering his control.

He found he could no longer be gentle. But it wasn't gentleness she craved. As he took the kiss deeper, her hands slipped beneath his sweater. She felt his involuntary shudder and thrilled to her newly discovered power. The flesh of his back was warm and firm. His muscles rippled beneath her fingertips as he unfastened the back of her silk dress. The fabric rustled in the silence of the room as it drifted to the floor. With steady hands he undressed her.

In a single motion, he tugged his sweater over his head. When her fingers fumbled with the snap at his waist, he helped her with sure, easy movements.

They clung, mouth to mouth, flesh to flesh. Pleasure slowly spiraled to passion. Passion became a fiery rage. There was no room left for thought, only feeling.

When their legs could no long support them, they fell to their knees, all the while murmuring incoherent words of endearment.

It was thrilling to explore the muscled strength of his upper arms and shoulders, the taut flesh of his flat stomach. She felt him shudder with need as her fingers moved over him.

His mouth followed the path of his fingertips as he learned the shape and texture of her skin. He heard her moan as his hand cupped a breast, and his lips followed, to nibble. Slowly, so slowly that it drove her to the brink of madness, he counted each small rib, then trailed her smooth flat stomach to the satin skin of her inner thigh. He was hungry for more of her, all of her. His fingertips were gentle, his tongue excitingly rough.

He heard her sigh his name as she urged his mouth back to hers, eager for the taste of him. Instead he took a slow journey, allowing his hands and mouth to savor her collarbone, her throat. Against her ear he murmured words she could no longer hear or understand.

She moaned and drew him to her.

For a moment longer he waited, loving the look of passion that clouded her eyes, softening all her features. Then he took her with him over the edge of sanity. She moved with him, her strength matching his. The intensity of their feelings drove them higher, then higher still. He sighed, whispering her name. And as she soared to a summit of pleasure, she couldn't give enough, share enough. She was liquid in his arms. If there could never be another moment in his arms, this would have to be enough. Enough to sustain her forever. She was his completely. And for the moment, Stefan was hers.

Chapter Thirteen

Kirsten's lids fluttered, then opened. She was lying in Stefan's arms, their naked bodies tangled in the sheets. She remembered being carried to the bed in the middle of the night. They had fed each other's hunger, slept, then awakened and made love again and again. Each time they discovered something new, something wonderful about each other.

In his sleep, Stefan sighed and drew her closer. His leg was flung carelessly over her. Protective. Possessive. It no longer mattered to Kirsten, as long as he held her.

If only they could stay here, she thought, trailing her fingers along his back. If only they could leave his world and hers behind, and hide away here in the villa. No public life. No private fears. Just two lovers, locked away from the world.

"Do I make you frown like that?"

She turned, loving the sound of his voice, husky from sleep. "Just thinking."

"Shouldn't do that. Bad for the complexion."

"Thinking?"

He laughed. "No. Frowning. You should think only happy, loving thoughts. I command it."

She smiled and brushed the hair from his eyes.

"That's better. Definitely better for the complexion. And better for my eyes, too. I love your smile." He leaned on one elbow and kissed the tip of her nose. "You're dazzling."

She loved the rough scratch of his beard. "Are you hungry?"

He gave her a wicked grin. "Starving."

As she started to roll away he caught her and pinned her beneath him.

With her eyes wide, she said, "I was going to order room service."

"It can wait." With one hand he swept her hair from her shoulder. "It isn't food I'm hungry for." As she started to speak, he interrupted. "Right now, I'd rather count your freckles."

"I don't have freckles," she said in her most haughty tone. "They're beauty spots. Gram told me."

Bringing his lips to her shoulder, he murmured, "She told you the truth. These are the most beautiful spots I've ever seen."

As his mouth began its gentle seduction, she felt the familiar stirrings deep inside her. He needed only to touch her and her body responded eagerly. They were like old, familiar lovers, she thought suddenly.

"Stefan." She gasped his name as he brought his lips to the soft swell of her breasts. Desire was swift, insistent.

"Sorry, love. Counting freckles—love spots—takes a lot of concentration."

"Umm."

As his fingers and lips began weaving their magic, she gave herself up to the pleasure of the moment. Running her fingers along his side, she located one of his sensitive spots and decided to do a tally of her own.

"How many sports do you teach?"

Kirsten looked up from the coffee she was pouring. It was afternoon, and they were just having breakfast. Time no longer seemed to matter. Neither of them had been willing to leave their bed long enough to eat until now.

"Baseball and track."

"I should have known. Both require endurance." He shot her a knowing look. "You've demonstrated that quality today."

"You're not in bad shape yourself."

He chuckled and helped himself to some grapes. "Soccer's my best sport. Tomorrow we'll have to challenge Michael to a game."

Tomorrow, she thought with a stab of pain. He still doesn't realize that tomorrow I'll be on a plane headed for home. She forced herself to show no emotion.

"He plays ball with some of the staff. Fancies himself quite a pitcher."

"I thought you were talking about soccer."

He grinned. "Michael thinks his game is baseball. With a ringer like you, I can finally beat that little monster at something. What's your specialty?"

"Pitching. I have a mean right arm."

He laughed in delight. "My smart brother won't be expecting to be bested by a skinny little woman."

"That's the second time you've called me skinny." She marveled at how normal her voice sounded. Stefan would never guess that she had to struggle at times to keep the conversation light and teasing.

"Sorry, love. You just look so fragile."

"I'm far from it."

"Yes. So I've discovered." Catching her hand, he lifted it to his lips. "Thank you for this day and night. It was a wonderful present."

She felt her eyes brim and looked away, embarrassed. "It's all I have to give you," she whispered.

He came around the table and wrapped her in his arms. Against her temple he murmured, "It's everything, Kirsten. I could never give you anything as fine as you've given me. You've made me so happy."

"No happier than you made me." I love you, she thought. I've never loved anyone as much as I love you. But why did the knowledge have to hurt so much?

"Had enough to eat?" His words broke through her reverie.

She nodded.

"Good." Catching her hand, he led her to the pool.

"We're going to swim?"

"Why not?"

"I don't have my bikini on."

"You don't need it." He began untying the sash of her kimono, all the while watching her face.

"What if someone sees us?"

He slipped the silk from her shoulders and allowed his gaze to trail her slender figure as her wrap drifted to the stone floor of the terrace.

"We're all alone in the universe, Kirsten. We can do anything we please."

She laughed, shaking her head, and he watched the way the sun turned the ends of her hair to flame. Fire. Every time he looked at her he felt the heat.

Dropping his robe beside hers, he caught her hand. "Let's see how much endurance you have in a pool."

He dived in a split second before she did. The cool water was a shock against her heated flesh. Coming up for air, she tossed her head, sending a spray of water about her. Her long hair drifted on the water behind her like a mermaid's.

"I'll race you to the far side," he challenged.

With sure easy strokes, she cut through the water. Beside her, he kept up with almost no effort.

When her fingers touched the side of the pool, she realized his were already there.

"You just have longer arms," she said, struggling for breath.

"Can't stand to lose, can you?"

She laughed and tossed her head. Water trickled in little rivulets down her face.

"No more than you."

"I see to it I always win," he said, laughing. "By making the rules to my advantage."

"Two out of three," she called. "We'll race again."

"No." Catching her by the shoulders, he drew her firmly against him. "I've thought of a new game."

His legs tangled with hers. Wrapping her arms around his waist, she felt her breasts flattened against his chest. Buoyed by the water, she felt oddly weightless.

Kissing the little droplets of water from her face, he whispered, "Your eyes put sapphires to shame." He moved his lips along her cheek, feeling her hands move against his flesh. "I'd like to shower you with jewels—diamonds, rubies, emeralds."

"I prefer daisies and chocolate bars."

"I've noticed." He moaned and drew her hips firmly against him. Passion built slowly, lazily, as their mouths clung, and their hands explored.

She felt her bones turning liquid, and she stored the memory. Back home, when her breath froze on the cold night air, she would remember these few languid days of magic and be warmed by the thought.

"You're going to drown me." She swallowed a mouthful of water, and he quickly lifted her above the water.

He took her hand and led her from the pool. Lifting her, he carried her inside and deposited her on the bed.

"I'm all wet," she protested.

"I'll dry you."

Dropping beside her, he wrapped his arms around her and ran slow, lazy kisses along her damp skin. For hours they lay tangled in the sheets, too lost in their lovemaking to care that the pillows bore the imprint of wet hair.

"Alexander and Anne Marie were a storybook couple."

Stefan was lying with his chin propped on a pillow. A sheet was tossed carelessly across his lower body. Kirsten was wearing his sweater. It fell to below her thighs. She had pushed the sleeves above her elbows while she straddled him, scratching and massaging his back. Each time she found a particularly sensitive area, he would stop talking and give a contented sigh.

"It must have nearly destroyed your father to lose them so soon after losing your mother."

Stefan nodded and gave another sigh of contentment as her hands continued their movement. "There was little left to identify after the crash."

Kirsten shivered. Almost tentatively she asked, "They died in an automobile accident, didn't they?"

"It was no accident. Investigators found evidence of a bomb. It had been planted in the engine of their car before they left the palace grounds."

Her hands stilled their movements. The breath seemed to have gone out of her. Her voice shook. "They were deliberately killed?"

"Assassinated. Our investigation still hasn't determined why. One theory is that someone wants to eliminate the royal family, one by one. That would weaken the will of the country."

Kirsten slumped down beside him, too shaken to react.

Turning, Stefan touched a hand to her shoulder. "I'm sorry, love. You're so easy to be with, I forgot for a moment that this is all new to you." Bringing her hand to his lips, he murmured, "We never released the results of the investigation to the press. We hoped the element of secrecy would be to our advantage."

Kneeling in the bed, she yanked her palm away. Her hands balled into fists. Her voice sounded strangely hollow. "Knowing this, you sent LeClerc away?"

"He made you uncomfortable," Stefan said easily.

"Uncomfortable?" Her voice turned to ice. "You'd risk your safety, your life, to make me comfortable?"

He saw her eyes narrow until they were tiny slits. Tears squeezed between the lids and rolled down her cheeks. Angrily brushing them aside, she shook her head, trying without success to stop crying. "Are you crazy? Can you actually be so careless about your safety?"

He stared at her, watching the flash of fury that seemed to turn her into a stranger he didn't recognize.

In a fit of uncontrollable rage, she began pounding her fists on his chest. "Your own brother was killed, and you sent your bodyguards away?" Again and again she beat her fists on his chest, tears streaming down her face. "You allowed yourself to be vulnerable, helpless—" her voice rose "—because I was uncomfortable."

Stunned at her outburst, Stefan caught her fists and held her firmly against him, while she cried out her pain and rage. Burying his hands in her hair, he stroked her head. His hands held, caressed, soothed, while she continued to rage. Finally the sobs that racked her body subsided.

When she grew still, he lifted her tear-stained face. His chest was wet with her tears.

For long moments she wrapped her arms around his waist, clinging to him. Then, reaching for the phone, she whispered, "Call your men."

Uncomprehending, he stared at her.

"Order LeClerc here immediately."

Gradually, his bewilderment became stunned comprehension. This woman, who valued her privacy more than anything, was turning her back on the very intimacy she craved. She cared so much for his safety that she was willing to share him with his men. She loved him. Though she hadn't yet admitted it, she loved him.

He cupped her face in his hands and kissed her eyes, her cheeks, her lips. She loved him. He swallowed the lump that threatened to choke him.

Punching the buttons of the phone, he waited, then spoke curtly. "LeClerc." While he waited, he continued staring into her eyes. When he spoke, he forced his voice to remain calm. "I want you to return. Now."

As he replaced the phone, he drew her firmly against him. Pressing his lips to the corner of her eye, he tasted the salt of her tears.

Against his throat she rasped, "Don't ever take that risk again. Ever."

He felt the little tremor she fought to control. "I won't. I promise you."

The phone on the bedside table shrilled. With one arm still around Kirsten, he lifted it to his ear. "Yes?"

Alana's worried voice responded. "Stefan, we've all been so concerned since LeClerc returned last night. Father's sending your car. He insists that you and Kirsten dine here tonight."

Stefan answered in a toneless voice, "Fine. Thanks, Alana."

Stefan felt Kirsten stiffen in his arms.

He lifted her face. Brushing his lips lightly over hers, he whispered, "You heard?"

She nodded.

"They'll be here within minutes. We'd better dress."

As Stefan walked to the shower, she slumped on the edge of the bed. She'd hoped to spend this last night alone with Stefan. Now even that would be denied her. She would have to share him, not only with his body-guards, but with his entire family.

Clasping her cold hands together firmly, she searched for the inner strength she'd always counted on in times of crisis. For a few brief hours, she'd been free to love him. She'd even entertained dreams of more, of a lifetime together. Now it was time to face reality. Tonight they would dine with his family. To-morrow, she would fly back to her world, a world that had no room for dreams and fairy tales.

Mechanically she slipped off Stefan's sweater and began to dress. Pulling on khaki camp shorts and a cotton shirt, which she tied at the midriff, she secured her hair with two combs, leaving the back to fall soft and loose to her waist. As she walked, it drifted about her like a silken cloud.

When a knock sounded on the door, she felt her heart stop. Stefan glanced across the room. Their gazes locked for one brief moment. Then he left the room. She heard the rumble of masculine voices in low conversation.

When he reentered the room a minute later, she had her nerves under control. Her hands, which still trembled slightly, were held stiffly at her sides. Her voice, when she spoke, was surprisingly firm. "Will you be leaving now?"

She was stronger than he'd expected. "It's only for a few hours. I'll need to speak to my father. Then, as soon as I've dressed for dinner, I'll be back to pick you up."

"That isn't necessary."

He crossed the room and gripped her upper arms almost painfully. His voice was low and angry. "I'll be here at seven. Be ready."

For our last evening together, she thought with a stab of pain. For an impersonal goodbye with all the family.

He kissed her, a hard, lingering kiss. Then he turned and pulled open the door. Just beyond it stood the grim-faced LeClerc. Their eyes met, and she felt the cold stab of steel. He blamed her for risking his prince's life, she thought with sudden insight. This man was a trained killer, whose only goal was to protect the man she loved. And he resented her for making Stefan vulnerable.

"Seven," Stefan said, breaking into her dark thoughts.

She nodded and watched as he strode to his waiting car.

She wanted to weep, but there were no tears left. Her savage outburst had left her drained. She ordered tea to soothe her nerves, and carried it to her bedroom, then went to her closet to pick out something special for her last dinner in Maurab.

Setting the buffalo on her bed, she gave a sad smile. Would she ever be able to look at his funny face without feeling all the joy and pain of these days?

Restless, she stood and paced. She needed to be busy, to keep from thinking. Walking to her closet, she went through the dresses hanging there. After a moment's thought she chose the same dress she'd worn that first evening. Pale ivory, the sundress had narrow ribbons that tied at the shoulders. The skirt fell in soft drifts nearly to her ankles. Laying it on the bed, she walked to the mirror and studied her image. That first night, Stefan had called her a mermaid. Taking the combs from her hair, she ran a brush through it until it crackled. She would wear it down for him.

Pausing, she cocked her head to one side. She had heard a slight shuffling sound from the patio, and a slow dreamy smile spread across her features. He'd come back. He was slipping in the way he always did.

With a little laugh, she dropped the brush with a clatter and ran to the terrace. "I knew you'd..."

All her breath seemed to be knocked from her. The stranger was short and stocky, all wide shoulders and bulging muscles beneath a straining T-shirt. But it was only the mask she saw. A ski mask had been pulled down over his face.

She froze, her eyes wide with terror. "Who...?" She couldn't put words together, couldn't think.

Darting a glance at the second masked figure behind him, she knew her only escape was through the front door. Spinning around, she started to run.

A hand clutched her arm. In her frenzy, she pulled free, unaware of the ripping sound as her sleeve tore away from her blouse. The front door. She had to reach it.

She was almost there. Her breath was coming in short spurts from the effort. Something, a stick or club, seemed to come out of nowhere. She was stumbling, losing her balance, falling. She didn't feel the blow to her head as she made one last desperate rush for safety. But she felt herself sprawling as she fell through space, and stars seemed to flash and dance in her brain. Pain engulfed her. There was a voice, low and angry, a great distance away. And then she knew only blissful darkness.

Stefan's hands weren't quite steady on the wheel. As if to assure himself, he patted the bulging jewelry case in his breast pocket and grinned in absolute delight.

She wouldn't take this gift gracefully. Too extravagant, she'd protest. And he would have to explain that every woman who'd married a crown prince of Maurab had accepted these jewels. Eight generations. Eight long, happy marriages, producing heirs for the throne. She would add a great deal of spice, and more than enough love, to the tradition.

It didn't seem fair that he'd told his father even before he'd asked her to marry him. But it had to be done. He had his father's blessing, as he'd known he would. In fact, his father seemed almost as joyous about the news as he himself felt.

Stefan smiled in the darkness and took a hairpin turn with a squeal of tires. Behind him, the black car followed neatly. She would insist that she had to go back to her class and finish out the term. He would persuade her to allow a substitute that honor. She would demand time to plot and plan, as women do before a wedding. And, he thought with a knowing chuckle, she would balk at the elaborate royal wedding his father would demand. But in the end, she would capitulate, because she loved him. She loved him. His heart swelled with the thought. He never would have believed he could be this happy. Flooring the accelerator, he drove the last mile in record time.

Stefan stepped over the low brick wall and crossed the terrace. The patio door stood open. He laughed softly. She'd known he'd come in the back way. A single light burned in the sitting room. The bedroom door was ajar.

Outside the door he patted the jewelry case in his pocket. He'd let her find it when she hugged him. Pushing open the door, he listened for some sound. It was ominously quiet.

On the bed, Buffalo Bill lay on his side. A white dress was laid out. Odd, he thought. She should have been dressed and waiting. A glance at his watch showed he was a few minutes early. She must be fixing her makeup in the bathroom.

"I'm glad you haven't dressed yet. Maybe I'll join you in a bubble bath before dinner."

When she didn't respond, he felt an uneasy prickle along his spine. A half-empty cup of tea stood on the night table. He crossed the room and felt it. Cold.

"Kirsten." In the silence, he hurried to the bathroom and threw the door wide.

The room was empty.

Spinning on his heel, he retraced his steps through the rooms of the villa. Empty. All empty. A razor of fear sliced his heart.

Methodically he began searching each room again. On the bed, set carefully beneath the stuffed buffalo, was a crude note. The words, pasted from magazines and news papers, read; "We have your woman. A ransom demand will be made soon."

A bitter taste of fury rose in his throat. Kirsten. His beloved Kirsten was in the hands of terrorists.

"LeClerc."

When the bodyguard hurried to his side, Stefan handed him the note. After scanning it quickly, the man meticulously went about examining each room of the villa. In the middle of the sitting room, he picked up a scrap of torn fabric from the floor and stuffed it into his pocket. Stooping near the coffee table, he touched a finger to a dark stain in the carpet. Instantly he returned to the bedroom and caught the prince roughly by the arm.

"They'll be phoning the palace with the ransom demand. You must be there for their call."

Stefan's head snapped up. "Yes. Of course. Get someone here immediately. I want these rooms gone over with a fine-tooth comb. Every thread, every hair must be examined."

LeClerc was already dialing the phone.

"It's done." His bodyguard led the prince across the terrace and to his car, skillfully avoiding the front room. There was no sense adding to his worry at this point.

As a swarm of vehicles converged on the villa, LeClerc drove the prince's car back to the palace. Beside him, Stefan turned bleak eyes to the swiftly gathering shadows along the highway. Who had Kirsten? What would they demand? Before, they'd killed not only Alexander, but his wife, Anne Marie, as well. Life meant nothing to these people. If they harmed her... If they hurt her in any way... His hands balled into tight fists. Without her, he wouldn't want to go on living.

Chapter Fourteen

Drink," the king ordered, handing Stefan a glass of brandy.

Having been notified of the crisis, the royal family was gathered in the library. One look at Stefan's harsh, angry features, and they became even more subdued.

Stefan downed the fiery liquid in one swallow.

Alana wrapped her arms around her brother's waist and rested her head against his shoulder, offering quiet solace.

Touching his brother's arm in a gesture of understanding, Andrew began to pace furiously. His hawklike features were taut. "Those bastards. We'll get them."

"How?" Grimly Stefan stalked to the window, staring at the darkness. "With all our power, with all the troops at our disposal, we don't even know how to begin to deal with them. I've never felt so helpless. If they've hurt Kirsten..."

It was Michael who appeared the most rational. "They can't afford to hurt her, Stefan."

"Why do you say that? Look what they did to..." Seeing the pain on his father's face, Stefan stopped himself.

"They need her alive and well if they're going to demand a ransom. And they know you'll ask to speak to her. You'd be a fool to do anything until you know she's all right."

Slowly Stefan nodded, seeing the truth in what his youngest brother said. Michael, the chess master, was always the logical one.

Restlessly Stefan paced. "Why don't they call?"

"Because they want us to suffer," the king said. "The longer we wait, the more our fears become magnified."

"Where do you think they have her?" Stefan's gaze swept the jeweled lights of the city. So many villas. So many hiding places.

"There are foreign ships and yachts in our harbors. I've alerted the navy. But there are also the mountains." The king sighed. "She could even be right here in the city, under our very noses." He touched his son's shoulder. "Michael is right, son. They won't hurt her."

"And the ransom?"

All his children turned to look at the king. Somberly staring into the fire, he said softly, "You know what our policy has always been regarding the paying of ransom. To give in to the demands of terrorists is to encourage even bolder attempts in the future.''

''We're not talking about government policy now. This is personal. Between me and the kidnappers. I have property, jewelry, a private art collection.'' Stefan's voice was equally soft and deadly calm. ''I'll pay any price, go anywhere, do anything they ask. All I care about is Kirsten.''

''And leave yourself open to harm?''

''It's because of me that she's been kidnapped. It isn't Kirsten they want. It's me.''

''All the more reason why you can't give in to their demands.''

''I won't discuss it. I'll liquidate everything. They can have anything, everything I own. They can kill me, as long as they release her.''

Storming to the liquor cabinet, Stefan poured himself another glass of brandy and drank it quickly. Warmth snaked through his veins, then settled low in his stomach. But it didn't ease the pain or erase the bitter taste of fear. Nothing would. His fists balled in impotent rage.

Kirsten lay very still, trying to absorb what had happened. She remembered muffled footsteps on the terrace. Stefan. No. Intruders. Masked figures, chasing her. She'd been running to the door, to safety. She'd almost made it. But something had stopped her. Something... Through a haze of pain, Kirsten blinked against the lamplight. She was lying on a narrow bed, on a cool cotton quilt. The ceiling was rough plaster in a pattern of swirls which resembled ocean waves.

Around the molding was an intricate design of boats and ships.

Moaning, she touched a cold hand to her forehead. It was swollen and tender. The hot poker of pain had subsided to a dull throb in her temple.

Across the room, a masked figure sprang from the chair and raced to the bedside. "Thank goodness, you're alive."

It was a girl's voice.

"I was afraid you might never wake up. He was only trying to stop you. But you tripped and hit your head on the edge of the coffee table. It was a nasty fall."

Kirsten studied the girl. Despite the mask, it was obvious she was hardly more than a teen. Her fine dark hair hung in limp tendrils. The skin of her throat and arms was pale, colorless. Through the holes in the mask Kirsten could see that her eyes were red. From crying or lack of sleep? While she spoke, the girl twisted her hands nervously.

"Where am I?" Kirsten asked.

Instead of answering, the girl handed her a damp cloth. "Here. There's dried blood in your hairline."

"Why have you taken me?"

"Money."

"I don't have any. I'm just . . ."

"We know that. You're a schoolteacher from the United States."

Kirsten felt her pulse race. "How did you know about me?"

"We have connections. We know all about you."

"Then you know that I can't pay you."

The girl laughed quietly. "Aren't you listening? We know everything. Even your... personal life. We are in need of money. A great deal of money. And since the royal family is too well guarded to get to any of them, we decided you were the next best choice. We have no doubt Prince Stefan will pay anything we ask."

Kidnapped. The realization sank in. Kirsten swallowed back the fear that threatened to choke her. What if these people had made their move while LeClerc and the other bodyguards were away? They would have caught the prize—the crown prince. She shivered. "I'm nothing to the royal family. A visitor in their country, nothing more. They won't pay your price."

The girl walked to the door. "We'll see about that."

A few minutes later Kirsten was dragged from the bed by a burly man in a ski mask. Another man, also masked, was speaking into a phone. He looked up.

Holding the phone out to her, he said thickly, "Your boyfriend wants to be sure that you're alive."

"Kirsten?"

She heard Stefan's low, angry voice and wanted to weep. Instead, she fought to keep her tone even. She clutched the phone so tightly that her fingers whitened from the effort. "Yes. I'm here."

"Are you all right?"

"I'm fine."

The phone was snatched from her before she could say more. As she was being dragged back to the bedroom, she could hear the man's voice growling, "Now if you'd like to keep your lady friend alive, this is what you'll have to do."

She was tossed back on the bed and the door was slammed shut. The girl sat down on the edge of her chair and watched Kirsten through narrowed eyes.

"Why are you doing this?" Kirsten needed to talk to keep from sobbing. She felt herself on the edge of panic.

"To cause the royal family pain," the girl spat.

"Why? What did they do to you?"

The girl twisted her hands in her lap. Though her voice was angry, her eyes looked frightened and a little haunted. "They cost my father his job. All because of a little money. Money they certainly didn't need. So now they're going to pay plenty."

"Did you—" Kirsten licked her lips and forced herself to show no fear "—kill Alexander and Anne Marie, as well?"

"That was an accident. They weren't supposed to be hurt. We only wanted to damage the garage and a fleet of cars. The bomb was set to go off early, before they left on their official visit. But something went wrong."

Kirsten felt the icy twist of fear. Accident or no, these people had killed. They were capable of doing so again.

"You may call it an accident. I'm not sure the courts would agree with you. Two people are dead because of a bomb planted by you or your people." Her voice lowered. "And now you're holding me against my will. If I die, will you call it an accident, too?"

The girl stood and paced in agitation. "Just do as you're told, and you won't get hurt."

"Is that what they told you?" Kirsten motioned toward the door.

"It's what I know." The girl's voice rose. "The prince will pay the ransom, and you'll be released unharmed."

As she unlocked the door and pulled it open, a man's voice could be heard from the other room. "Where do you think you're going?"

"Outside for some air." The girl slammed the door.

Kirsten heard the key turn in the lock. Then there was silence.

Sitting up, she began to examine her surroundings. Besides the small bed there was a dresser, two chairs and a writing desk. On one wall was a blackened stone fireplace. The picture hanging over the mantel was a portrait of a handsome young boy. He looked vaguely familiar, reminding her of someone she'd met recently. This was a child's room. The furnishings were old and of very good quality. The owner of this place had a background of wealth and culture. Was the owner involved in this kidnapping? Or was this a rented villa?

Dragging a chair to a small, high window, Kirsten peered out through narrow iron bars. Below her was a winding street, outlined by streetlights glistening in a lightly falling rain. Across the way, she could see the lights illuminating the pink stucco wall of a neighboring villa.

Her heart raced. She was still in the city. Craning her neck, she strained for a glimpse of the palace. It was just out of sight above the hills.

Stefan. So close. She blinked back tears. And yet she might never again see his beloved face.

As she watched, the headlights of a car moved slowly past. Freedom was just a few feet away, just beyond these barred windows.

Hearing the scrape of the key in the lock, she quickly jumped off the chair and hurried back to the bed. By the time the door opened, she was reclining among the pillows that she had propped against the ornate headboard.

"Your prince is getting the money together." The girl's throat was flushed with little spots of color. Sarcastically she added, "You must be special to him. He's agreed to pay a million dollars for your release."

Kirsten detected the note of triumph in the girl's tone. "And then what? What will happen after he pays you what you've demanded?"

"You'll go free." The girl's lips curled into a thin smile.

"And you? Will you ever be free again?"

Instantly the girl's smile fled. "With a million dollars we'll have a chance to start over. My father says my brother and I will have enough money to live wherever we want."

Her father and brother. Did the girl realize what she'd just revealed? Kirsten filed the information away. The fact that they were one family would make them easier to identify. Kirsten had to keep her talking.

"How can anyone raise a million dollars in cash?"

"I don't know. And frankly, I don't care." The girl shrugged. "Let him sell off some of the family jewels and paintings. They should belong to the people, anyway.''

"Is that what your father told you?"

"Yes. He said..." The girl seemed to catch herself. "I don't want to talk anymore. My father told me to stay here and watch you."

"Where has he gone?"

"He's gone to make certain the prince follows through on his promise. He still has a certain amount of influence in the government." With that, the girl turned her back on Kirsten and sat down stiffly in a chair.

"You have an interesting accent," Kirsten said conversationally. "Where did you go to school?"

"If you speak to me again, I'll have my brother come in here and gag you. Do you understand?"

Kirsten didn't reply. In the silence, her mind whirled. What had Gram always said when things went wrong? "Never dwell on what's wrong in your life; instead, concentrate on what you have to do to make it right. Talents, girl. We all have 'em. Most of us don't use the half of 'em."

When the girl left the room again, Kirsten began rummaging through drawers and cabinets. There had to be something here she could put to use. Talents. What were her special talents?

It was well past midnight. Lights blazed in every room of the palace. Though he vehemently disagreed, the king had accepted his son's decision to accede to the kidnappers' demands. Now Stefan was astounded at the speed with which doors that would have otherwise been closed to him were suddenly opened. The king had called in his council of advisers. They had unanimously agreed with the prince. Even Henri Soulier, who could usually be counted on to cast the dissenting vote, agreed to the ransom payment. Leaning heavily on his cane, he had risen to speak eloquently about the need to buy the young American's freedom. The bank chairman had been brought by chauffeured limousine to the palace, where he had been apprised of the situation. He personally assured the prince that the ransom money would be available as soon as the vault opened the next morning.

At last the king ordered the staff to retire. In the library, the family waited in grim silence for the kidnappers' final instructions. Two military men stood at attention just outside the door. At the desk, the head of the government security forces fiddled with a recording device attached to the telephone. Three advisers carried on a muted conversation on the other side of the desk.

Alana huddled in a high-backed chair drawn up by the fire. Across her lap was a richly embroidered mohair throw that one of the maids had provided. Occasionally she darted a glance at the stony profile of her brother.

Andrew, consumed with nervous energy, paced. He'd been pacing for hours. For a while earlier, he'd gone to the palace gym to work out his frustration. Then he'd returned, to be with his family. To wait. To pace.

The king stood silently at the window, staring at the darkened outline of the city. His city. His country. His people. It was natural for a man in his position to have made enemies. His hand clenched. He found himself raging against a coward who would hide behind anonymous phone calls instead of coming forward to take responsibility for his actions.

Michael sat quietly at the chessboard. Slowly, methodically, he played both sides. It helped to keep his mind from the real war being waged.

Stefan held a gold lighter to the tip of his cigarette and inhaled deeply. On the desk, the ashtray was littered with the remains of crushed cigarettes. Was she crying? Was she hurt? Afraid? His thoughts were driving him mad. Once she was safe, he'd deal with his anger. Right now, all he cared about was Kirsten. It was fear that drove him. Fear. A feeling completely alien to him until now.

The shrilling of the phone shattered the silence. Stefan grabbed it before the first ring subsided. Anxiously his family gathered around him.

"Yes."

"Do you have the money?"

"It will be available at nine o'clock. I want to talk to Miss Ste—"

The caller cut him off abruptly. "I will call at exactly nine-fifteen to tell you where to take the money. At that time you will get your final instructions."

"Let me speak with Miss Stevens."

"In the morning."

The line went dead. The technicians shook their heads in defeat. There hadn't been time to trace the call. Wearily Stefan replaced the receiver before lifting his gaze to the others.

Kirsten finished the sketch of the girl in her mask and studied it carefully. It was a good likeness. When the key turned in the lock, she folded the paper and stuffed it under her shirt. By the time the door opened, the pencil had been hidden under the pillow, and Kirsten was sitting on the edge of the bed.

"Brought you something to eat." The girl set a tray down on the dresser top.

"I'm not hungry."

"Better eat. It'll be hours before you're out of here."

Kirsten fought to hide her excitement. "When will I be set free?"

"When we get the money. Bank opens at nine. If everything goes right, we'll leave word where to find you after we're safely out of the country."

If. If, Kirsten thought. If there were no mistakes, she might be found in hours or days. Her breath caught in her throat. If anything went wrong, she might never be found at all.

Her mind raced. She needed to be alone. Touching a hand to her forehead, she moaned softly.

"What's wrong?" The girl's tone showed genuine concern.

"My head aches. I don't feel well." Kirsten lay back against the pillow. "I need something. Aspirin."

The girl hesitated a moment, then drew the key from her pocket. A minute later, Kirsten sat up quickly as the door closed and the lock clicked.

While she'd been drawing, a plan had been forming in her mind. She had to let someone know where she was. From the lights burning in the windows of the villa across the way, she knew that someone was living there. She had to take a chance that it wasn't someone connected with the kidnapping.

From beneath the pillow she extracted the small baseball she'd found under the bed. On the bottom of the sketch, she wrote a quick note. Carefully wrapping the drawing around the ball, she secured it with rubber bands she'd found in the desk. Standing on a chair, she opened the window and studied the iron bars. Her aim would have to be perfect if she was going to miss the bars and still hit the window of the villa across the street. All her concentration, all her energy went into this one, critical pitch. As her ears strained in the darkness, she heard the distant tinkling of breaking glass.

Snuggled beneath the mohair wrap, Alana slept fitfully. Still seated at the chessboard, Michael struggled with the missing pieces of the puzzle. By now he should have figured out who was holding Kirsten and why. But the logic of the kidnapping eluded him. Perhaps that was why he couldn't put it together, he thought. There was no logic to this cruel act. Shoving himself away from the chessboard, he hurried toward the servants' quarters. Maybe the staff had picked up some interesting bits of gossip.

Andrew had returned to the gym in the basement of the palace, where he could take out his anger on the punching bag.

Stefan and his father sat on either side of the desk, talking softly. At times, the king knew, his son's mind wandered to the woman he loved. Alaric could only watch helplessly as the prince struggled with building frustration.

When the phone rang, both men stared at each other in surprise. Glancing at his watch, Stefan muttered, "It's too..." With an oath, he jerked the phone to his ear.

"Yes?"

He listened to the voice on the other end while his father strained to make out the words. Alana threw off her blanket and hurried to stand beside the desk. In the next instant Michael was there, too. He had just put together bits of gossip that told him who could be behind the kidnapping.

Writing furiously, Stefan thanked the caller and warned him to do nothing until he was given official orders.

When he hung up, he pressed a button on the desk. Within seconds, the door opened to admit LeClerc. Behind him, Andrew came running sweat pouring down his flushed face and neck.

No one spoke. Stefan's eyes glittered a little too brightly. In a carefully controlled voice he said, "Kirsten managed to get a message out."

"How? Where? Is she all right? Is she on her way?" Everyone except LeClerc was shouting.

Holding up his hand, Stefan demanded silence. "She is being held in the Soulier villa."

In the stunned silence that followed, no one seemed able to speak.

"How do you know this?" It was LeClerc.

"That was a neighbor of Soulier's on the phone. He said a ball was hurled through his window, along with a note from Kirsten saying she was being held there and a drawing of one of her captors. I don't understand what's going on." Stefan shrugged. "All I know is that I intend to get there right now and see for myself."

"You must call the military," the king protested.

"And have her injured—or worse—when the soldiers advance on that villa?" Stefan shook his head and stood resolutely. "I'm going there myself."

"And I'm going with you," Andrew insisted.

"Me too." Michael moved to stand beside his brothers. "I just heard from a source in the palace that Soulier expects to come into a large sum of money. I want to be there when we capture that bastard."

"Wait." LeClerc touched the prince's arm.

Everyone looked up at his quiet, commanding tone.

"You cannot be involved," he said softly. "None of you. Until we know whether this is a larger conspiracy, you owe it to your people to stay where you can be protected. This is my job. And I do it well."

Stefan seemed about to protest. The king touched his shoulder. "LeClerc is right. We would only complicate matters. You can't go, Stefan."

He knew the pain his words caused, but the only outward sign Stefan gave was the violent clenching of his fists. Lifting his gaze to his bodyguard's, he whispered, "Keep her safe, LeClerc."

The man's eyes never wavered. "Count on it."

He spun on his heel and strode out the door.

"I'll catch hell from my generals," the king muttered, dropping an arm about Stefan's shoulders.

If LeClerc fails, Stefan thought, I'll suffer the pain of hell for all eternity.

The figure scaled a low wall and melted into the shadows. With his face blackened and a dark sweater and pants tucked into black boots he blended easily into the trees and shrubbery surrounding the villa.

Moving silently, he paused every few feet to listen. Finally he heard the sound of muffled conversation. Pulling himself level with a high window, he peered cautiously over the sill. Two men were smoking. The gray-haired one had his back to the window. Resting beside his chair was a cane. Facing him was a young, dark-haired, stocky man wearing a workman's coverall. On the table beside his chair lay a skier's face mask.

"To Australia. From there we can hire a yacht. There are hundreds of islands where a man can stay lost for as long as he chooses."

LeClerc's gaze swept the room, noting the automatic weapons on the table. To the left of their chairs was a closed door.

Dropping lightly to the ground, he moved quickly around the building. Pulling himself up again, he peered through the bars into a much smaller room. In a chair facing him was a thin young woman wearing a mask. She was staring intently at the bed. His gaze followed hers. Lying on the bed, her eyes focused on the window, was the object of his search.

With a professional eye, he scanned the room. The girl in the chair didn't appear to have a gun. He wished she'd stand up. Then he'd know better if she had a weapon concealed on her person. The young woman on the bed looked alert, composed. She wasn't crying. Her voice was strong. She seemed to be trying to engage her guard in conversation. Ignoring her words, he looked beyond her. The only exit was the door. Testing the strength of the bars on the window, he found them unyielding. It didn't leave him much choice. He had to confront the armed men.

The thought of death didn't frighten him. He faced it every day of his life. What did worry him was the innocent young woman on the bed. He'd have to keep her out of any cross fire. Regardless of the cost, Kirsten Stevens had to escape unharmed. He'd given his word to his prince.

Chapter Fifteen

Kirsten saw the shadow at the window and blinked. She paused for a single heartbeat, then forced herself to continue speaking in a normal tone. The shadow disappeared. She waited, hoping to see it again. The light from a solitary star winked in the blackness. Had there been someone, something there? Or had it been her imagination?

"What's wrong?"

She realized she'd grown silent. "Nothing," she lied. "Just my head. It still hurts."

"The aspirin should have eased the pain by now." The eyes behind the mask glowered at her.

Kirsten swallowed and fought a wave of despair. What if no one had been home when she'd tossed the ball through the window of the neighboring villa? What if it was still lying there, undiscovered?

She had to keep the girl talking. "You say your father is angry with the royal family. Does that mean he knows them personally?"

The girl blinked at the sudden shift in the conversation. "All his life. They always had more. More privileges. More power." Her eyes narrowed. "After my mother died, my father began visiting the casino. Soon he was there every night. His gambling debts were more than he could ever manage to pay. When his creditors demanded payment, he went to the king." She stood and began to pace. "Do you know what our precious king did?"

Kirsten shook her head, wondering if the girl realized just how much she was revealing.

"He told my father to sell our villa and live more modestly." Her voice rose. "Sell the property that's been in our family for generations."

"What did your father expect?" Kirsten asked.

The girl's voice betrayed all the pain and rage she felt. "He expected an old family friend to offer his help. The royal family could wipe out our debt without making any sacrifice at all. Instead, we're expected to give up the only home we've ever known."

"Won't you have to give it up now?" Kirsten said softly. "When you collect the ransom, won't you have to flee your home forever?"

She could see shock register in the girl's eyes. In a subdued tone, she said, "Maybe. But at least we'll be able to live in style. My father has promised never to gamble again."

"I'd call this the biggest gamble of all," Kirsten muttered.

"Be quiet. Listen. What was that?" The girl leaped to her feet.

Kirsten sat up. She'd heard it, too. A muffled sound.

"Is everything all right in there?" The girl paused a moment with her ear to the door. When there was no response, she took the key from her pocket and opened the door.

As soon as she disappeared, Kirsten ran to the open doorway. The outer door was hanging by one hinge. In the adjoining room, one of her captors lay beside an overturned chair. The younger kidnapper was struggling with someone. They turned and she gave a gasp of recognition when she saw it was LeClerc.

While the two men struggled, the girl darted around them to reach the weapon on the table. Seeing where she was headed, Kirsten shouted. "LeClerc. Behind you."

He turned, and with one sweep of his arm, knocked the girl to the floor, where she crumpled in a heap. But the distraction had given the kidnapper a reprieve. Making a dive for the table, he grabbed the automatic weapon and turned it on his attacker.

"Don't move," he ordered.

With the muzzle of the gun pressed to his chest, LeClerc froze.

Behind them, Kirsten had no time to think, only to react. In one swift motion, she scooped the cane from beside the unconscious kidnapper and wielded it like a baseball bat, swinging it at the head of the armed man.

For one instant, LeClerc grimaced, expecting to be shot. Instead, he watched the man drop heavily to the floor. Stunned, he stared at the slender woman standing over the gunman, her arms poised to strike again.

Kneeling, he plucked the gun from the man's hands, then gave her a half smile. "Lady, I'm glad you're on my side."

Her laugh came out in a shaky little sigh. "Am I ever glad to see you."

Seeing her knees buckle, he grasped her firmly under the arms and led her to a chair.

"Put your head between your knees. It'll pass."

"I've never fainted in my life." She tried to sound haughty, but the words were muffled and breathless.

"I have." He pressed her head down gently, then walked to the phone. A moment later, she heard him say, "All clear. Send someone to pick up the trophies." He paused, then held the phone toward her. "Say something before he tears the phone out of the wall."

She took the phone. "Stefan? I'm fine. What? Oh—" she smiled weakly at the man who towered over her "—just practicing my baseball."

More than a dozen vehicles converged on the villa. While soldiers and police looked on, the royal family rushed inside.

"Kirsten." Stefan caught her in a bone-crushing embrace and hugged her fiercely to his chest. "Are you all right? Did they hurt you?"

"No. I'm fine. Really," she said as he held her a little away.

"They hit you." Touching a finger to her temple, he saw her wince. "I'll kill . . ."

"Stefan, it's just a little bump. I ran. The younger one chased me. The other—Henri," she amended, "must have tripped me with his cane. I hit my head on the edge of the table, I think."

"We'll have it looked at immediately."

She smiled and touched a hand to the dark stubble of his beard. "You look awful."

"And you look wonderful." He pressed her to him, then reluctantly released her as his family gathered round.

"Oh, it must have been a nightmare," Alana murmured, feeling the sting of fresh tears.

"It's over," Kirsten whispered, brushing Alana's tears gently. The concern of Stefan's family touched her deeply.

"The bastards," Andrew said savagely, as he gave her a bear hug.

His father touched his arm to caution him. "Control yourself, Andrew. You're in the presence of a lady. And for heaven's sake, let the poor girl breathe."

As she gave a little laugh, the king drew her into his arms. "We've been so worried. And we're so grateful to LeClerc. We owe him your life."

"I'm afraid you have it wrong," the bodyguard said.

Everyone turned to look at him.

He gave Stefan a broad smile. "It was Miss Stevens who saved my life. One of the kidnappers was holding a gun to my chest. If she hadn't knocked him out with that cane, I'd be a dead man now."

The king slapped Stefan on the back. "What did I tell you? Breeding always shows."

Stefan swallowed back his laugh at the sight of Kirsten's arched eyebrow.

"She's a scrapper," the king said proudly. "Just like her father. A war hero, you know."

"Ah, yes. About that investigation. I'd like to tell you exactly how I feel about . . ."

Stefan pressed his fingers over Kirsten's lips to stifle her protest. Turning a smile to his father, he said, "I think maybe Kirsten's more like her grandmother. A tough old bird, I've heard."

The family's laughter died as they watched the three kidnappers being led from the room.

Stefan's hands balled into fists. "I never trusted Henri. But my father was kind to him. Rather than discipline him, he gave him another chance. And this is how he showed his gratitude."

Beside him, Kirsten caught his hand. "Stefan," she whispered, "it's going to be punishment enough for him to see his own children paying for his terrible mistakes."

The royal family grew silent as the three kidnappers were taken away for questioning. Security forces began going over the rooms, recording every shred of evidence.

The military had surrounded the grounds and were posting sentinels until the work was completed.

Leaning heavily on her father's arm, Alana said, "I don't want to stay in this place. I can't stand thinking about Kirsten being threatened here, where we once played as children."

The king nodded and led her toward the car. Michael and Andrew followed in subdued silence.

Watching them, Stefan caught Kirsten's hand and brought it to his lips. When she lifted her eyes to his, she saw the weariness etched there.

"I've had a lot of time to think, Kirsten," he said softly.

"So have I."

"I don't want you to interrupt while I say what's on my mind."

With a little smile, she acquiesced.

"I know you think my life is too confining. And I know you hate the thought of bodyguards and attack dogs and the military. And I have no right to ask you to share a life you find so distasteful. But I can't help myself. I have to ask you. Because the truth is, I can't bear to think about living here without you. I love you, Kirsten. I thought I'd die worrying and wondering about you. And if you leave me, it'll be worse than death."

As she opened her mouth, he added harshly, "I know you have a job to do in the United States. But it's possible to find replacements, even in the middle of the school year. And I know you won't always be happy sharing your home with so many brothers and a sister, plus a father-in-law, not to mention dogs, cats, maids and valets. But think about it. Don't say no too quickly."

"All right."

"Don't deny how you feel. Despite all our differences, I know we could make it work."

He stopped talking long enough to notice her smile. "Did you just say what I thought you did?" he asked.

Kirsten laughed. "You're so busy giving me all these arguments, you haven't listened. I've had a lot of time to think, too. All I prayed for was the chance to see you once more, to tell you how much I love you. Stefan, all my life I've been alone. I can't think of anything nicer than sharing your father and sister and brothers. I've discovered how much I care about all of them. They're a wonderful, loving family. The kind I've always dreamed of."

"And the bodyguards?"

She glanced at LeClerc standing attentively in the doorway. "They're willing to lay down their lives for someone else. I don't know how anyone could show greater loyalty, or greater love."

"You'll stay and marry me?"

"Well, there is one favor I'd ask you."

He drew her close, feeling the fire begin. "Anything."

She grinned. "I'd like Frank and Rose and Amy here for the wedding. They're like family. Besides, Amy's never seen a real live handsome prince. This will be better than any fairy tale."

"I'll go one better. Why don't we fly in your whole second-grade class for the wedding? I think they should see their Miss Stevens marry her prince."

"You'd do that?"

He thrust his hands deep into her hair and nuzzled her temple. Sparks were igniting all around them. Any moment now he'd be on fire. "Kirsten, I'd do anything in the world for you."

"Really? Anything?"

At his nod, she wrapped her arms about his neck and whispered, "Would you mind sending LeClerc away?"

"Won't you ever learn?" He grinned. "Actually, I was just thinking the same thing. Are we both crazy? After what we've all been through?"

Against his lips she murmured, "You could just send him outside. Send them all outside. Then we wouldn't have to waste another minute."

He pulled her firmly against him feeling desire begin to pulse and throb. Lifting her easily in his arms, he rubbed his lips over hers. "I have a better idea. My car is just outside. I know of a great country place where we can shut out the rest of the world. Of course—" he laughed "—you'll have to put up with a few crabby kittens."

"Not to mention a staff of hundreds."

"Only dozens."

"Only dozens? I think I could learn to enjoy being cared for by dozens of people. How long will it take you to drive us there?"

"Only minutes, love. We can wait that long. Especially since we'll have the rest of our lives to love each other."

As he carried her outside, she breathed deeply, enjoying the heady fragrance of gardenias that filled the air. Bringing her lips to his throat, she sighed. "You know we're going to live happily ever after, don't you, Stefan? Like your friend Marcella said, it was written in my palm. You and I can't escape it. You were my destiny."

He felt his heart swell with emotion. For the rest of his life he'd be thankful for the gift he'd been given. "And I can't think of a more wonderful fate than you."

Silhouette Special Edition

COMING NEXT MONTH

FORGIVE AND FORGET—Tracy Sinclair
Rand worked for the one man Dani hated—her grandfather. And though Dani knew it was just Rand's job to entertain her, she found herself falling in love with him.

HONEYMOON FOR ONE—Carole Halston
Jack Adams was more than willing to do the imitation bridegroom act, but he didn't want to stop with an imitation, and Rita wasn't willing to comply. She wanted someone serious and stable, and Jack was anything but.

A MATCH FOR ALWAYS—Maralys Wills
Jon was a player without a coach; Lindy was a coach without a player. They made an unbeatable team so it was only natural they would find each other. Suddenly tennis wasn't the only game they were playing.

ONE MAN'S LOVE—Lisa Jackson
When Stacey agreed to help Nathan Sloan with his daughter, she didn't realize that the father would be the biggest puzzle—and cause the most problems.

SOMETHING WORTH KEEPING—Kathleen Eagle
Brenna was unsure about returning to the Black Hills, but nonetheless she was excited to compete against Cord O'Brien. She was confident she could win the horse race, but she might lose her heart in the process.

BETWEEN THE RAINDROPS—Mary Lynn Baxter
Cole Weston was hired to prove that Beth Loring was an unfit mother. But how could he build a case against this woman when he found himself falling head over heels in love with her?

AVAILABLE THIS MONTH:

DOUBLE JEOPARDY
Brooke Hastings

SHADOWS IN THE NIGHT
Linda Turner

WILDCATTER'S PROMISE
Margaret Ripy

JUST A KISS AWAY
Natalie Bishop

OUT OF A DREAM
Diana Stuart

WHIMS OF FATE
Ruth Langan

Silhouette Desire

**Available
January 1987**

NEVADA
SILVER

The third book in the exciting
Desire Trilogy by Joan Hohl.

The Sharp brothers are back, along with
sister Kit...and Logan McKittrick.

Kit's loved Logan all her life and, with a little
help from the silver glow of a Nevada night,
she must convince the stubborn rancher that
she's a woman who needs a man's love—not
the protection of another brother.

Don't miss *Nevada Silver*—Kit and
Logan's story and the conclusion
of Joan Hohl's acclaimed
Desire Trilogy.

ATTRACTIVE, SPACE SAVING BOOK RACK

Display your most prized novels on this handsome and
sturdy book rack. The hand-rubbed walnut finish will

Buffalo, NY 14269-1325

Offer not available in Canada.

BKR-2